NO MAN

OF

Woman Born

ANA MARDOLL

This book is a work of fiction. Names, characters, locations, and events are products of the author's imagination. Any resemblance to actual persons, living or dead, business establishments, events, or locales is coincidental. The author acknowledges the trademarked status and trademark owners of the word marks mentioned in this work of fiction.

NO MAN OF WOMAN BORN by Ana Mardoll
Copyright © 2018
All rights reserved.

ISBN: 978-1-9874129-1-8

Published by Acacia Moon Publishing, LLC
Cover illustration by Anna Dittmann
Audio narrated by Cori Samuel

Books by Ana Mardoll

THE EARTHSIDE SERIES

Poison Kiss (#1)
Survival Rout (#2)

REWOVEN TALES

Pulchritude
No Man of Woman Born

CONTENTS

Author's Note

Fantasy novels were my escape as a child. On cold or rainy days when the world closed in around me and my chronic pain flared up, I hid under my pink duvet clutching a library book and read until my troubles were forgotten. *Peter Pan*, *The Chronicles of Narnia*, *The Lord of the Rings*, *Dragonlance*, and Piers Anthony's *Xanth* series formed my childhood; the complete works of Patricia C. Wrede (which had been banned from my household as the 'wrong kind' of magical fantasy for good Christian girls to enjoy) were my first purchase when I moved from my parents' house into a place of my own. Talking dragons and magical witches and daring swordsmen were everything to me, and carried me through good times and bad.

My first attempts at creative writing were based in fantasy worlds, yet every time I started a new work the project would stall. For all that I loved high-fantasy settings, I didn't feel I had anything to add. My focus shifted to fairy tales where I could explore domestic violence in my 'Beauty and the Beast' retelling, *Pulchritude*, and to urban paranormal in my *Earthside* series where I write queer and disabled protagonists who escape from abusive situations to find freedom and a supportive community whose members who share their marginalized identities. In short, I wrote where I felt my voice could have the most impact, and high fantasy remained on my reading stack for pleasurable escapism only.

What I hadn't anticipated when I set out to change the world with my writing was how much my writing would change me. Between publishing *Poison Kiss* and *Survival Rout* I realized the transgender and nonbinary gender characters I'd included in my fiction carried within them large parts of myself. I came out as trans to my friends and a weight lifted from my shoulders. All the messy, confusing, complicated gender feelings I'd carried with me for so long had a name, a label, and a community—I wasn't alone and I wasn't the only one. I was happier than I'd ever been.

After the heady rush of coming out had passed, I looked at my reading stack and saw with a pang how often I wasn't included in those fantasy worlds. I spent many a night peering at *The Lord of the Rings* and wondering who among the cast (possibly Merry?) I could imagine as a genderfluid demigirl with neopronouns like mine. I realized I *did* have words I wanted to add to the fantasy genre. I set aside the *Earthside* draft I'd been working on and started a new project. I would write stories *I* needed to read, each with a transgender character who was the hero of their own tale. My words would be chosen for fellow trans people seeking escapism; I didn't want to provide 'Gender Theory 101' or write big 'coming out' discussions for each character. Their gender would be the same as for cis characters: real, valid, and affirmatively theirs.

I wanted to write the stories I'd needed as a trans child hiding with a book under a pink duvet.

No Man of Woman Born is the name both of this collection and one of the stories within. The title comes from a trope of prophecies in fantastical settings wherein an event which seems impossible nevertheless comes to pass because of a loophole in the rule. J.R.R. Tolkien is popularly (and possibly apocryphally) believed to have created the character of Éowyn (shieldmaiden of Rohan, and slayer of the Witch King of Angmar who 'can be killed by no man') after being irritated by Shakespeare's weak resolution to the 'no man that's born of woman' prophecy in *Macbeth*. After all, if no man born of woman can accomplish a given task, that seems like an excellent time to bring in a woman to do the job, rather than introducing a man who isn't *born* of a woman because he was 'from his mother's womb untimely ripped'.

Whether or not this origin story for Éowyn is true, the tale has stuck with me. Éowyn was one of the first female characters in a fantasy setting I read as a child, and was formative in many ways for me. She dressed as a man and rode to battle as a man and fought as a man, but she was no man herself. She proclaims her gender on the battlefield— *"But no living man am I! You look upon a woman."*—and everyone believes her. She doesn't have to argue or explain or justify herself; she simply states what her gender is and is not.

Éowyn is written as a cis woman, of course, and this is a privilege cis people have that trans people do not in our society: the privilege to have one's gender accepted and not considered a matter for debate. Yet what if she were not cis? What if she were assigned female at birth like me, but neither a man nor a woman? What if she were both? What if she were a trans woman and the prophecy knew even if those around her didn't? Where were stories about *those* characters: trans heroes and heroines whose genders broke, subverted, and fulfilled prophecies as neatly as Éowyn's gender fulfilled the prophecy about the Witch King of Angmar?

The stories I've written here do just that: break, subvert, and fulfill the same gendered prophecies that cis characters have encountered since the dawn of storytelling. The heroes and heroines in these pages aren't special *because* they are trans; they are special *and* they are trans. They face trials and tribulations as any character does, and emerge triumphant. No trans character is killed in the pages that follow, none are deadnamed, and misgendering is kept to a minimum. The assigned genders at birth of the nonbinary characters are not revealed unless necessary. Trigger warnings are provided before each story, as well as pronunciation guides for neopronouns used by nonbinary characters. Wherever possible, I have tried to make this collection accessible to trans readers, with cis audiences welcomed but not centered.

These are stories I needed to read, sent out into the wider world for anyone else who might need them too.

TANGLED NETS

Content Note: Violence, Bloodshed, Community Ableism, Sacrificial Victims, Self-Sacrifice

Neopronoun Pronunciation Key: Xie ("zee" or /ziː/), Xer ("zur" or /zɜr/)

M ist rolled over the bay in the wake of the summer storms, bringing a wet chill that seeped through every crack and soaked each blanket. The bitter morning wind forced Wren to bundle up in xer second set of clothes before leaving the hut to lug xer fishing nets down to the grass-speckled hill overlooking the bay. Perched on xer favorite rock, xie worked until xer fingers were chapped numb from the cold ocean spray, repairing holes and strengthening the weave of xer nets while the sun crept over the horizon.

Wren could work by feel now, leaving xer eyes free to wander over the jagged waves and their white peaks whipped to a dancing frenzy by the wind. Yet no matter how often xie tried to look away, xer eyes were always drawn back to the gray cliffs ringing the bay and the dark gash cut into the stone high above the line where the sea stained the rock a brackish green. In rare moments when the wind died, Wren could hear the white dragon slumbering in that dark cave. Ponderous snores marked the massive bulk of the creature, each lung in its chest the size of the small human shivering on the rocks below.

Despite the bite in xer fingers, Wren didn't mind the work. Routine was calming, a distraction from the coming winter and its heralding fog which blanketed the village in silent dread. No matter the weather or week, xie hiked to the hill laden with nets, sat on xer rock, and let xer fingers fly over the thick webbing that had kept Wren alive and fed from birth. Mending a tear here, reinforcing a spot there, xie made the nets ready to be stretched like a fence along the ocean floor where they would entangle the strongest swimmers.

When the sun shook herself free of the horizon and just before the village fishers poured down the hill, Wren rowed out in the battered community rowboat to bring up nets xie had placed the day before. Xie sorted the haul, threw back the smallest, and set repaired nets in place for the next day's catch. Light danced on the water as villagers who could afford boats of their own began to row out to join xer; those who couldn't waited impatiently for Wren to row back to shore, wet netting lumped in xer lap and fish flopping over xer feet.

On land, Wren wrapped the haul in xer nets and lugged everything back up the hill and through the sparse forest that cradled xer family home. There xie sorted the catch a second time, deciding what to cook, what to trade, and what to store. The ritual of filleting the fish was calming, the sharp edge of xer knife flashing in the midday sun. Lunch was set on a pan over the fire to fry while Wren hung strips of flesh in the tiny drying shack opposite the hut door. Xie carried embers from the hearth to smolder in the base of the shack; the smoke would ward flies away, while heat and wind dried the meat for winter.

The routine was comforting in its familiarity, designed to store enough food to keep the family alive over the coming winter months. But everything had been easier when Dwynwen was still with them; her fingers had flown over the nets like a stone skipping the bay, and when they took their catch down to the village to trade she had bargained with the devil's own quick tongue. In the wake of her loss, there were now only two mouths to feed but the amount of work had not lessened.

Their mother, Eirlys, did what she could to help but was habitually sickly. Whenever illness confined her to bed, she could rise only to tend the drying shack and stir dinner. She had never recovered from Wren's birth, and her health sustained a second blow at Dwynwen's death. Eirlys had slumped insensible to the ground during those final rites, wailing feverish curses as her daughter of seventeen summers was led in procession to the valley. Wren had helped her walk back to the hut afterwards, xer mother's arm slung over her youngest child as together they struggled with each step.

On that first night back, Eirlys slept dead to the world. Only with great difficulty had Wren been able to wake her and coax down a small portion of the grain Dwynwen had bought for them. Dwynwen wouldn't want them to waste her sacrifice, and Wren repeated this until Eirlys weakly acknowledged the truth. The grain had been good for her and she'd rallied, leaving her bed in short bursts to clean the hut. She hiked monthly to the valley, visiting the little grave they'd dug for Dwynwen's braid. Sitting beside the wooden grave-marker, she sang songs or wove flower garlands to leave on the tiny dirt mound.

Over time, however, the visits brought her more pain than comfort. She fell ill again and missed a month, then another. After she recovered, she never visited the valley again. Now, almost four years to the day after Dwynwen's death, Eirlys was ill once more. Wind slipped through cracks in the hut walls to lay icy claws at her throat. Wren watched her from the doorway, pausing when xie stepped inside to pull lunch from the fire. Eirlys lay on their only bed, wrapped in every blanket they owned and still shivering.

Xie told xerself she would be fine. Sickness rose from the shoals every year, endangering infants and elders, yet Eirlys always recovered. She was stronger than she looked, her frail body beating back disease time and again. Wren would go down to the village and trade with merchants for goods: livestock bones to make a heartier broth than could be coaxed from fish, and medicine made from the herbs that clung to the rocky hills surrounding the valley; precious things paid for in fish and oil. Xie would be forced to dip into their winter stores to afford these luxuries, but the alternative was unthinkable.

Wren couldn't let Eirlys die, even if others would. Xie glared fiercely at the speculative whispers which had begun to trail xer whenever xie went down to the village. The villagers lived in fear of the changing seasons, and were hungry to hear that a lottery would not need to be held this year. They had a knack for sniffing out sickness, like wild hill dogs circling a flock in search of its weakest member. But they could not have Eirlys. If Wren could have xer way, they would never again have *anyone*. No creature should suffer Dwynwen's fate, and no one should be forced to endure what Wren and Eirlys survived.

"Hallowed day is coming."

Wren knew right away xer tone of voice was wrong; xie sounded too defiant. Xie had intended to sound calm, even grateful. Supplication and humility were appropriate in xer position, not anger. Yet the terse words were free in the air with no net to catch them, so Wren set xer shoulders and stood like a tree.

If the mayor noticed, nothing showed on his face. He sighed where he sat on the long bench at the head of the common building, shuffling papers around the table like pieces in a game. "It is, yes. Already the autumn harvests are coming in. The Dyers had an especially good year. It always seems to go that way, doesn't it? When the fishers have a bad year, farmers thrive. When the farms struggle, fish leap into the boats. I suppose we should be grateful we don't all starve at the same time."

He paused to make a mark on one page, his spidery handwriting covering the precious sheet with inky tracks. If Wren knew how to read the markings, xie would see the names of the farmers with numbers representing the wealth of their harvests. A nearby basket contained stones and shells, each with a hole bored in the center and strung with knotted thread to represent fishing hauls over the year. These knots and numbers added up in an arcane way to the portion each house owed the community. The yearly tax wasn't high, but was enough to feed a single desperate family facing the prospect of a hard winter.

Wren's token was a simple black stone, hollowed out years before by Wren's father and identical to the ones used on xer nets as weights against the ocean current. Other families marked their nets and hauls with decorative shells—xie knew at a glance the flashy white ones for the Mannerings and delicate pink ones for the Brownes—but common stones had been all Wren's family could ever afford. Wren didn't mind this, at least not when xie could avoid thinking about it. Now was not one of those times.

"I want to volunteer. I want to be the sacrifice."

Only now did the mayor look up at Wren, blinking rheumy eyes at xer. "Say that again, child?" He frowned, rubbing at his chin and leaving a streak of watery ink where his thumb grazed the leathery skin. "You're hardly old enough to volunteer."

"I'm seventeen summers." The same age as Dwynwen when she'd had this conversation, but Wren pushed that thought away before it could show on xer face. Sacrifices must know their place and maintain decorum. Eirlys' wails during Dwynwen's final rites were excusable; after all, it wasn't unusual for family members to lose themselves in grief. However, it wasn't appropriate for Wren to be angry four years later, xer rage nurtured like an ember against the dragon, the lottery, and the villagers who escorted xer sister to her death. Xie struck an obedient expression and tried again. "I'm old enough, sir."

"Seventeen already?" The mayor hummed and hawed, stroking his jaw. Despite his protests, there was no official age limit. The dragon wouldn't accept children if they were too small, but villagers as young as fourteen had gone in procession to the valley. The qualification wasn't age so much as the ability to make a satisfying meal. Wren was big enough, which meant Wren was old enough. Xie waited as the mayor's eyes took on a faraway look, reminiscing over times long past. "Can you believe I remember your birth as though it were only a season ago? Your poor mother was in labor for two days. How is she doing?"

"Poorly." Wren shifted on xer feet, uncomfortable standing but not wishing to sit on the bench. That would be too intimate, sending a signal that xie wished to stay longer than the time necessary to conclude xer business.

"That's a shame," the mayor said, his brow knitting into a tighter frown than before. "But all the more reason why you shouldn't volunteer, child; Eirlys needs you. After your father and sister died, you're all she has left. Are your food stores low? If that's the case, my wife and I could spare a little. And if Eirlys is truly ill, I'm sure she'd much rather give herself than—"

"*I said*, I choose to volunteer. Sir."

Xer abrupt words hung in the air between them. The mayor blinked, unaccustomed to being so rudely interrupted, and ran a hand over his eyes before responding. With an insight unaccompanied by guilt or pity, Wren realized that the old man was trying to be patient with xer.

"Wren." He reached out to take Wren's hand; xie tried not to blanch, but the texture of his palm was as dry as sea salt. "I know you took your sister's death hard, child. And I *am* sorry to hear Eirlys is ailing."

"She'll be fine." Xie would make certain this was true.

The mayor ran his thumb over xer hand and Wren had to fight not to draw back. "Eirlys has lived a full life. You are young, with your own life ahead of you. Do you believe she wants to see you throw that away?"

Anger flared within xer like a stab of lightning striking the sea. Wren yanked xer hand away, unable to bear his touch a moment longer. "What life? Surviving under the shadow of that creature? Sorting the daily haul and worrying each time whether we'll have enough this year to pay for someone poorer than us to die? Selling my own mother like a fish at market and walking with her in procession while I tally the reward in my head?" Xie would spit if it were not for the floor. "*No*. I won't help send another person into the valley; not her or anyone else."

The elderly man frowned, his thick jowls set with anxious concern. "Wren, be reasonable! There's no shame in paying the tax! And no one is going to force Eirlys down to the valley! I was only saying that *if* the alternative is starvation, I'm certain she'd rather it were she than another of her children!"

"It's me. I volunteer. I want to be the sacrifice." The urge to leave was unbearable, and Wren longed to step back into clean open air. "I'd rather die than participate again. I won't be a part of what happened to... her." Dwynwen's name was on xer lips but xie couldn't speak it; she was too precious to share.

The mayor sighed, staring dejectedly at his papers as though they could answer him. "I can't deny your request. If you are determined to volunteer, the other families will see your will done no matter what I want. All I can promise you is timely payment, and my vow to care for Eirlys when you are gone. Won't you reconsider, child? At the very least, sleep on it before you decide. We have several days yet."

"My mind is made up." Xie whirled and stalked out of the hall, xer boots slapping the floor with every step.

Halwen was there when xie returned to the hut, though Wren hadn't sent for her. She stooped over the fire, her back hunched on the left side. Wren had never seen her stand perfectly straight though she must once have been able to do so, long ago when she was a girl and her scraggly hair was some color other than gray.

She had come to tend Eirlys, for Halwen was a witch who could set broken bones, treat illnesses, and deliver healthy babies when they turned in the womb and midwives said there was no hope. She read signs in the stars, predicted the ocean's moods, and sometimes told pregnant villagers whether they carried a boy or a girl before their belly even began to show. Her predictions were never wrong.

She didn't look round when Wren entered but her voice rasped at the touch of xer foot on the doorstep, the gravel in her throat making Wren's own itch in sympathy. "Brought honey-tea for her to drink. Soothes ache left by the cough. She's sleeping now. Stew's on the fire, with herbs that will help fight sickness."

"What do I owe you?" Wren's words were abrupt to the point of rudeness, xer tone strained from arguing with the mayor and now anxious at the prospect of indebtedness to the witch. Halwen had never directly harmed their family but the sight of the old crone stung, bringing painful history into the hut with her.

When Eirlys had been pregnant with Dwynwen, Halwen placed a hand on her stomach and declared the child "a girl, but an ill-fated one." Her prediction had hung like a cloud over the sunny child, whose ill fate seemed to be a lifetime tending her sickly mother while her father fought to keep the little family fed. When a scrawny newborn followed a few years on Dwynwen's heels, Halwen touched Eirlys for the second time, tilted her head, and said nothing at all. It was bad luck when a witch refrained from pronouncement, and some said the baby would come soon and die young. Wren tried xer best to do both, yet the midwives saved the tiny infant.

Dwynwen became a second mother to Wren, who didn't speak a word until five summers old and who preferred the silent ocean to the village square. No one else knew what to make of the reclusive child, but Dwynwen understood Wren perfectly. She played with xer by the seashore, pretending to be pirates or bandits or even the white dragon itself for Wren to slay. If her fate as the eldest child in a family of poor fisherfolk seemed ill to others, she didn't seem to mind. They were humble but happy until Father died, Mother worsened, and the dragon took Dwynwen away, sealing her ill-fated end and proving Halwen right after all.

Wren resented the witch's failure to prophesy a happier future for xer sister, but Halwen was untouched by xer animosity. She uttered a barking laugh at Wren's question of payment. "Gratitude would be nice, child," she observed, gripping her cane of knotted wood for support as she bent to stir the steaming pot.

Xie watched her with wary eyes, feeling like a bird tensed to fly. Halwen always called Wren 'child' but not in the same way the mayor did, as though xie were too young to matter. The word in the witch's mouth wasn't condescending; it simply filled a space nothing else could fill. If Wren hadn't been so predisposed to mistrust the meddling woman, xie might have taken pleasure in the neutral appellation.

"Gratitude doesn't warm old bones."

Halwen shook her head, amusement in her dry crackling voice. "You never were much for niceties, child. Have you considered becoming a witch? We can get away with such things. Well, since you're determined to be generous, that silver-scale you've left to dry on the line outside caught my eye. Third from the pole."

Of course she would demand the prize of Wren's daily catch. Yet despite xer annoyance, Wren felt a rush of palpable relief. Xie could pay this now and be done, without the threat of future payments to hang over xer head. The price was dear, but the witch could have asked for much more.

"It's yours." A long pause stretched as Halwen studied the fire, making no move to leave. "Thanks," Wren added, the word bubbling up with belated delay and an awkwardness no one could miss.

She chuckled and poked at the smoldering logs in the fireplace with the tip of her cane. "You always were an odd one, Wren. Even before you were born." She paused to peer at the embers. "No, that's not quite right; not odd, but different."

"I'm *me*." This time xie didn't care if the words came out surly.

"You are. We are all ourselves." The crone lifted her chin to fix Wren with a piercing gaze and xie flinched as xie always did. Halwen had witch's eyes above her broad flat nose: one a rich nutty brown and the other clear as water. "Why, look at me," she said, her lips curling into a toothy smile. "*I* am a witch."

With effort Wren forced xer gaze back up to Halwen's, staring with unblinking eyes at the witch like a dying fish caught in xer own nets. Xer voice dropped to a whisper, giving voice to a question xie would never have dared to ask had not xie just arranged xer own death. "What's it like, being born a witch?"

Her laugh was silent this time, a snort of air that stirred the white tendrils of hair framing her wrinkled face. "I see the world through different eyes, child, as do we all." She tilted her head, studying Wren as if xie were a tangled net and she were looking for the best place to begin. "I will tell you what few are old enough to recall: I was not born a witch. I was made a witch."

A frown knit xer brow; xie had never heard this before. "How do you make a witch?"

Halwen smirked, her unmatched eyes glittering with the unholy mischief Wren had held as lifelong belief must have been ingrained at birth. "Cook my payment for our dinner, child, and I will tell you a tale."

"The white dragon went bad more than a century before I was born." Halwen sat outside with Wren, her voice quiet so as not to disturb the sleeping woman within the hut. She gnawed the last bits of flesh from a fish bone as she spoke, plainly satisfied with her payment for the evening's work.

Wren sat beside her with xer nets in xer lap, freshly fed and returning instinctively to the daily chore which had guided xer mornings and nights for as long as xie could remember. Though xie had accepted xer own death, the ritual of untangling and repairing these nets had kept xer alive for too long to be set aside now. Xie worked in gathering darkness as the setting sun dipped her toes into her nightly ocean bath and shed her clothes to spread vermilion across the tree-studded sky; Wren needed no light for xer familiar task.

"When ships still launched from the harbor?" Already Wren could feel xerself being caught up in the story despite xer mistrust; ancient ships and their wind-fattened sails were a favorite of xers. As a child, xie begged Dwynwen to tell tales about the wrecks which lay at the bottom of the ocean outside the bay. Wren liked to fancy that any driftwood they found was the hull of a long-forgotten vessel, and xie would come running to watch whenever the dragon hauled up golden chains or ropes of pearls from the deep. These were lost treasures of an older time, scavenged a century after sinking to line a cold wyrm's nest.

"And our kingdom had a king, yes," Halwen answered, the wisp of a smile on her face. "They say the dragon guarded the northern borders of our kingdom as part of an agreement with the king and his kin. But which king had brokered the deal and which king had broken it, and whether those two men were the same man, was fiercely argued among the old-timers in the village square. No one knew, you see; they'd all been children when the dragon first attacked, and no one remembered the initial grievance."

Wren knew dragons lived longer than human memory, unweathered by time's passage. An angry dragon couldn't be outlasted like a storm; it would do no good to huddle together in the common building until the lashing winds quieted. Nor was there safety in retreat, for they dwelt everywhere. Red dragons filled the eastern skies at night, hunting both sheep and shepherd as their giant membranous dragonfly wings beat the air in a rhythm so fast the eye caught only a blur. Black dragons infested the southern forests, their sleek wingless bodies wrapped around tall redwoods. Thrice the length of a human, they hunted large game: deer, boar, and bears which ambled along the shore dipping paws into the water for fish.

The white dragon was the largest of its kind, with thick leathery bat wings and sly intelligence gleaming in its ancient eyes. It was too proud to circle hills at night in search of fat sheep, and too broad to slink between trees. Instead, its hunting grounds were the western waters and their endless depths. The dragon attacked the waves, soaring high enough to pierce the clouds and flinging itself into the sea. When it surfaced after a span of time longer than any human could hold their breath, its claws clutched fish no net could contain: big meat-eaters that never ventured into upper waters. These leviathans were carried back to its lair as food, and the humans who dwelt below considered themselves lucky to be too insignificant to hunt. All the dragon required of them was a yearly token sacrifice for the privilege of living in its shadow: one human life, delivered to the valley.

"By the time I was born, things had settled into a routine." Halwen's voice was soft on the evening breeze. "The lottery was held after autumn harvest, which was always in need of as many helping hands as possible. We drew lots and the unlucky one was taken to the valley. There was no resistance. Every family had been touched by that first attack, and we children and grandchildren were taught from infancy what the dragon was capable of: humans hoisted into the sky and dropped into the village square like sacks of fish."

"But you must have thought about it." Wren leaned forward to peer at the witch, xer netting momentarily forgotten. When xie had been little, Dwynwen played the dragon and Wren would slay her time and again, always trying out some new tactic. As xie grew the fantasy deepened, the filleting of each day's catch taking on new meaning as xer knife sliced through flesh and bone. "No one tried to kill it, even once?"

"No one in the village." Those unmatched eyes glittered with dry amusement. "We had our share of adventurers even then, of course."

Wren sat back in disappointment, xer hands returning to xer work. Adventurers were not xer favorite subject. They came to brave the northern cliffs, drawn by tales of the dragon's gold. They claimed a desire to free the village from its terrible tribute, but Wren saw the greed in their eyes. Xie would watch them climb the dizzying mass of jagged rock while xie mended

12

nets or drew in the day's catch, waiting for their broken bodies to be hurled into the sea below. The dragon rarely bothered to eat such nuisances.

Once one of their number tangled in xer nets and Wren suffered a shock when pulling in the catch. The corpse surged up from the water in front of xer face, its dead eyes accusatory in the morning light. In xer dreams, that body became Dwynwen. Her hair was short after they'd cut away her braid to bury, and wet strands stuck to her face. For weeks after the dream Wren suffered panic when hauling in the nets, expecting to see xer sister's face even though the fear was irrational. Dwynwen wasn't in the bay; Wren had been in the valley with the other witnesses when xer sister disappeared down the dragon's gullet.

"Then the soldiers came." Reminiscence flickered in Halwen's eyes as Wren snapped back into alert interest. "The last king was long dead, and his generals had fractured the country into tribes and factions while my father was still a young man. But the queen's youngest daughter tried to hold the line. Keep peace, mend factions, stop the warlords. She sent soldiers north with orders to kill the dragon."

"To protect us?" Wren leaned forward, scarcely daring to breathe.

Halwen chuckled. "So they claimed, though my father said they came to take its hide and claws and teeth as trophies to rally the troops, thinking the battle would be good training for new recruits. Their general thought the battle would be easy; he was accustomed to the little green dragons that dwell south of the forest. 'Big as a bride and half as dangerous,' my father used to say. Not like our white monster."

"But they tried?" Feral eagerness clawed xer stomach, hungry for any scrap of detail. "What happened?"

"They came the day of the lottery. I had drawn the white stone from the bag. Yes, I was the sacrifice. I was only thirteen summers, but I was big-hipped and big-breasted and the elders said I must draw with everyone else. My father was furious. He threatened to take us south but my mother's wiser head prevailed; if we weren't eaten by dragons, we'd be captured by slavers. I had readied myself for death when the soldiers marched in, swords at their waists and helmets gleaming like the ocean. I thought they were my saviors."

Wren could barely breathe, straining to see Halwen in the dark. "They had a seer with them. An elderly woman with sad blue eyes speckled with brown moss. She placed her hand on my head and told me I had a gift. My eye changed when she touched me, though only I knew it then; the color didn't drain until the next full moon, long after she was gone. My father said she had an evil gaze, and locked me in my room."

Halwen shook her head, her breath forming white puffs as she spoke. "But I *saw*. Alone in my room, I watched that army scale the cliffs, their bright swords flashing in the sun. We still have one of those swords. My brother fished it out of the bay afterwards. Father hung it on the wall and polished it every night until he died. I didn't touch it after that. It's rusted over now, as red as the blood that coated it that day."

"They died." Wren needed to hear her say it, xer fingers clutching the nets like a lifeline.

"Every last one of them." Halwen tilted her head back to find the moon, his cold light filtering through the trees. "The dragon laughed as it snapped their bones, and in my mind's eye I couldn't turn away. We could hear its boasts all the way down to the village, crowing that no man nor woman would ever kill it, nor beast nor fish nor fellow dragon. My mother said I screamed the words in unison with the creature, but I wasn't aware of doing so. If I did, that must have been my first prophecy; it has never proven false."

Xer breath stuck in xer throat as xie leaned forward in xer seat. "But that doesn't mean it can't be killed, does it?" In xer voice was all the anger xie couldn't display before the mayor. "Even if its boast were true, even if your words were a prophecy! There are people— there *must* be people who aren't—"

Wren's voice trailed away as piercing eyes turned to study xer. "Who aren't *what*, child?"

14

Soldiers and seers had been helpless before the dragon, but they had been men and women. Wren was neither, yet the knowledge did not make xer feel special. Xie simply was xerself, in the same way Halwen was a witch. Xie had resolved to face death so Eirlys might live, but now xie could not help but wonder if there might be another way. Xer fingers flexed in the nets, tightening and relaxing in an anxious rhythm.

A thought nibbled at the corner of xer mind, like a fish at xer toes. "You didn't die. You weren't sacrificed."

"Lucky me." Halwen's lips turned up in a humorless smile. "The dragon demanded the mayor as penance for allowing the army to come. My father's brother took over the post and my father suggested the tax as a replacement for the lottery. Poor families always died over winter, and everyone agreed that was a tragic waste of human life. So the village instituted a levy on all harvests and hauls, the proceeds to be given every year to one willing sacrifice; someone whose family wouldn't survive the winter without it. Death by dragon was faster than starvation, and the rest of the family would live. One death to save many."

Wren winced and looked away, unable to meet the witch's eyes. "Families feed off the corpses of their loved ones." Xer voice was bitter as smoke. "The dragon ate Dwynwen, and we snatched up the scraps."

Not a lick of pity crossed the witch's face, only that faint ever-present amusement. "Death is inevitable, child. Nothing escapes it forever; not you, not me, not even a dragon."

Xie snorted and stood, brushing xer hands on xer knees. Inside the hut, xer mother shivered under a pile of thin blankets; she needed Wren's clothes laid over her for warmth. Wren was wasting time and heat out here, listening like a fool to an old woman spinning tales. "If I'm going to die, I'd rather die trying," xie told Halwen, dismissal lacing xer hard voice. "Better to die doing something worthwhile than live off the dead."

The stew seemed to help Eirlys. She slept more peacefully and coughed less often in the days that followed, though she wasn't fully mended by hallowed day. Wren walked to the village on the morning of sacrifice with a guilty tread. Xie knew it was cowardly not to say farewell, but the alternative of sending her into a feverish faint was worse. Better to let Halwen tell her after the deed was done. She would eat the grain Wren's sacrifice had bought and she would survive. Wren could give her that much.

Villagers waited in the square, gathering nervously in the dim dawn light. Wren watched their faces relax as xie emerged from the line of sparse trees which dotted the hills around xer hut. A hand reached out to lightly grasp xer forearm and xie forced xerself not to shrug away the unwelcome touch. There was a ritual to observe, and it was as much to assure the villagers that the chosen sacrifice would not run off as it was to comfort the doomed soul and their grieving family.

Dwynwen had gone through the same ritual. She'd held Wren in her arms and hummed softly as her long braid was cut away as a token for the family to bury. Farmer children wove a straw crown while Wren leaned into her shoulder and tried to memorize the warm spring scent she always carried. She was dressed in a white gown donated from one of the village families, so that Wren and Eirlys would not be poorer for the loss of Dwynwen's clothes. Xie remembered how the white gown glowed pink in the light of that final sunset.

Now that it was Wren's turn, xie submitted to these ministrations with less grace. Xie kept xer own threadbare clothes, knowing they were too thin to be of any use to Eirlys. Xer hair would not be cut since xie had never been patient enough to grow it out. Wren wore xer longest boning knife in a belt at xer waist; an unusual choice for a sacrifice since the tool would be lost forever, but it was xer right to go to death dressed as the fisher xie had been in life. Embracing the role, xie wore a cloak of thick netting that tumbled down xer back and swept the ground as xie walked. Wren had touched these nets daily almost from birth and was determined that they accompany xer in death. Eirlys would not need them, but xie did.

16

When they led Wren down to the valley, the sky was already streaked with pink. Winter was coming on fast, shortening the days as the sun fled from the bitter northern winds. The shortest day was marked as a holiday, a holy day when no work would be done and every able-bodied villager turned out of their homes to honor the chosen sacrifice and their solemn procession to the valley. A soft susurration of crying spread through the village as Wren walked with the mayor and representatives from the village families, the ritual sound cresting above the constant crash of ocean waves. Xie wondered for whom they were crying.

They waited in the valley for the dragon to appear, all eyes turned to the darkening sky. When it emerged from the gash in the cliffs, white scales stark above the black sea, it spread its great wings with the same unhurried ease as a cat stretching and leaped into empty air. After circling twice in long lazy loops, it swooped down to land in the very center of the verdant depression cut into the coastal hills. The creature's feet slammed into the ground with an ostentatious *whump*, and the villagers drew back with a chorus of gasps; yearly familiarity couldn't lessen the awe inspired by its imposing presence.

Wren stood forward from the crowd in front of the village elders. The creature's gaze transfixed xer, binding xer in place as the mayor cleared his throat and began his speech. Words flowed over Wren without touching xer, the sentiments as familiar to xer as the folds of netting xie rolled between xer fingers. Over and again, xie touched the braided ropes which had been xer inheritance and livelihood as all the while unblinking orbs stared at Wren, the way wild cats watched for scraps when xie filleted fish.

When the mayor concluded his speech, a hush stole over the clearing as the villagers watched the dragon and the dragon watched Wren. Wings spread wide against the dying sun, the creature wore the gray-white hue of a fish too long dead. Talons on each paw flexed in the dirt, ready to reach for Wren and carry xer back to its lair. The creature breathed, a rumble building in its throat to a roar, and the husky voice that emerged could never be mistaken for anything human.

"I accept your sacrifice, humans. You may safely live and hunt in my territory for another year."

Wren gripped the edge of xer cloak tighter, the folds of rope heavy on xer back. Xer heart pounded in xer throat but xie would not scream. Xie refused to let them see how hard xer heart was beating or how fast xer thoughts were racing. The valley felt too cramped, packed with more humans than Wren could count in knots and the monstrous lizard hunched in the center of them all. White teeth gleamed at Wren as its mouth split in a grotesque smile, and in that moment xie was certain that it could smell xer fear.

In the absolute worst case, it would hurt. Death would hurt and xie would be gone and Eirlys would be alone with her grief and enough food to feed a family of five for a year. She could ration what would keep and trade what wouldn't and she would find ways to survive without Wren. That was the worst case.

In the best case, however, xie could do as xie had imagined so many times as a child, playing countless games with xer patient sister as xie slew in a hundred different ways the monster who dwelt above them. Xie could do this because no one had ever tried before, and because a dragon tensed and ready for an adventurer's step into its cave was *not* the same as a dragon squatting lazily before an assembly of cowering villagers, waiting for the ceremony to be over so it could carry its yearly snack back to its lair.

If Halwen's prophecy were true, Wren could do this because xie was neither man nor woman. Xie was human and whole, but different from the others. Wren was xerself.

Scales on one forearm tensed to move and Wren knew this was the moment. In xer childhood games xie had spoken—a declaration, a challenge, a shout of defiance—but now xie made no more noise than an oar dipping into water. Xer hand tightened on the edge of xer cloak and xie stepped forward, whipping the nets from xer back and twirling them wide over xer head as if readying to cast them out over the sea. The dragon blinked at the unexpected movement, but its pride would not let it rear away from the tiny human.

Wren's fear was gone now, shoved to the back of xer mind as something to deal with later. Xer arms knew what to do and xer mind followed: lift and twirl and cast wide, hurling the heavy nets free of the boat that wasn't under xer this time. The netting fell with a thick slapping noise on the great lizard, its wings beating wildly in instinctive outrage at being pinioned. This thrashing only entangled the creature further, the jagged tips of its wings poking through the netting as ropes tightened against delicate leather.

"Stop, child! What are you *doing*?"

Xie could barely hear the mayor under the furious roar. The nets were sturdy, having been made strong under xer careful attentions all these years, but were no match for a dragon. Wren snatched the knife from xer belt, fingers closing around the worn hilt of the boning blade. A deep swallow of air, a glance at the creature's thrashing feet, and xie dove to the ground to scramble forward on arms and elbows towards its smooth belly. Xie angled the knife and jabbed the curved blade up into the chest of the writhing monster.

Wren was rewarded with a hot splash of blood that stung xer eyes and coated xer hands so slickly that xie almost lost the knife. Xie tightened xer grip and continued crawling, blocking out the roars that assaulted xer ears. The knife dragged a long cut in the wake of the initial wound, but Wren knew from a lifetime of nicks that the slice was more irritating to the creature than genuinely painful. That was fine with Wren. Pain didn't matter; what mattered was the liquid life spilling to the ground as xie steadily widened the wound.

Screams rose, human wails filling the air in confusion and panic; feet trampled the valley as people stampeded away from the enraged creature. Wren heard bodies hit the ground as the dragon's tail lashed wildly and struck unlucky bystanders, and xie caught glimpses of others dragging the wounded away from danger. Beneath its legs, Wren watched the thrash of the flailing tail and hesitated; it wasn't safe to stay under the beast, but neither did xie believe an exit lay that way. Making a quick decision, xie slammed xer knife high into the wound and left it there as xie rolled sideways between its legs.

Nets grasped at Wren as xie rolled away, but xie knew their touch and how to move under them without being caught. Xie scrambled to xer feet the moment xie was free of the ropes, dancing back from the dangerous paws digging furrows in the once-grassy valley. The creature was trying to cut itself free, but its claws were made for stabbing instead of slicing and its efforts only drew the ropes tighter around it. Wren was reminded of a wild cat that had caught itself in xer nets once when hung out to dry; xie hadn't been able to free the creature until it wore itself into a calmed state and xie could approach.

The dragon was more intelligent than a cat, of course, but Wren had made time its enemy. Blood stained the muddy ground and more dripped out at an alarming pace; eventually it slowed, but not in the way a bleeding cut slows as it heals. The dragon was dying, and the baleful eye that turned on Wren seemed to understand this. Xie was no expert on the emotions of dragons, but xie thought it looked more shocked than angry.

"I did it. I killed the dragon." Xer numb whisper had barely enough breath behind it to escape xer lips. On xer tongue xie tasted the blood that coated xer from top to bottom. "I did it for you, Dwynwen." And for Eirlys, and anyone else who might otherwise have walked in procession to the valley. Wren's hands were not free of blood, but no one else would ever die in xer place. "I did it."

The dragon, now more red than white, staggered under the clinging nets. One paw moved to clutch at its gaping chest, but there was nothing to be done. The creature slumped to the ground, its eyes locked on Wren to the last until those unblinking orbs glazed over in death. Stillness crept over the valley as the young fisher stood drenched in blood and shivering in the night air. Wren heard distant wails from the villagers tending to those wounded by the dragon's thrashing but xie felt a warm sense of solitude, as if everything in existence had shrunk to xerself and the motionless body beside xer.

Halwen was the one who found Wren as she walked with her cane down the trampled path humming an old sea shanty to herself. The moon had taken his place as lord of the night, his silver light turning the red blood on the ground a watery black. The old woman picked her way to the trembling youth and threw a heavy cloak around xer shoulders—not netting this time, but real fur. Soft and still warm from a hearth, the article brought life back to the motionless survivor.

"I've got to get home to Mother," xie murmured. Xer voice felt changed somehow, thick and heavy in xer throat. Xie coughed and winced at the pain in xer ribs. A bone was broken, or at least bruised, and would need attention. "Do you have an extra cane I could borrow? And maybe something for the pain? I'll pay you another fish. Not a silver-scale, but I have a red-tail you might like."

The witch's unmatched eyes glittered in the moonlight. "Come along, then. My, but you *do* like to do things the hard way. Do you realize that dragon's blood has turned both your eyes quite black? There are easier ways to become a witch, you know. Lean on me, child, and we'll get there together."

KING'S FAVOR

Content Note: Border Walls, Population Purges, Violence, mention of Self-Harm
Neopronoun Pronunciation Key: Nee ("nee" or /niː/), Ner ("nur" or /nɜr/)

Caran's plan hinged on passing through the kingdom of Northnesse without drawing notice, for those who caught the attention of the witch-queen were rumored not to live long after. Worse still from the perspective of ner employers, if nee were captured and interrogated then future expeditions would be compromised. The last thing the Magic Guild wanted to contend with was tightened border security.

Nee had spent the autumn harvest season traveling on back roads and sleeping under the stars whenever nee could, staying in villages only when ner supplies needed replenishing. The back roads were better for ner purpose and less populated; the fewer people nee spoke to, the less ner accent could be remarked upon. Nee affected Northnesse mannerisms as well as nee could, but there were always words and phrases nee did not know, language quirks which had evolved in the time since the borders had been closed to foreigners.

As winter approached, it was now time to leave; Caran would not be able to sleep outside in safety for much longer and nee had no desire to tempt fate by settling in a village for an entire season. For better or worse the expedition was over, and the guild would have to be happy with the information nee had obtained; no more would be forthcoming until they supplied money and necessities for another incursion.

Leaving Northnesse was risky, but far easier than entering. When the witch-queen rose to power and closed the borders, incoming visitors were subjected to a harsh vetting process before being allowed entrance into the kingdom. Yet those who chose to flee elsewhere were for the most part allowed to funnel through the Eastborne wall, provided they left behind most of their worldly belongings for the crown to seize. Caran had spoken with refugees in Freyhurst before setting out on ner expedition and knew what to expect when nee arrived at a checkpoint: a small line of impoverished farmers seeking relief elsewhere, mixed with a few merchants permitted to cross the border on business, and capped with a modest military presence to maintain order.

Each checkpoint along the Eastborne wall lay at the heart of a city or town which fed and housed local guards. Caran selected a middling-sized town for ner approach, hoping to find a small gathering of refugees fleeing the coming winter. Nee hoped to blend into their ranks as just another hungry mouth seeking better fortune on the other side of the wall, slipping out of the country with few questions asked.

Instead nee found nerself walking deserted streets as eyes peered from the windows of every house. No children played in the yards framing the main thoroughfare, and no merchants called from their doors to advertise fresh bread or local wine. The town was silent and this unnerved Caran; the villages nee had passed through during ner expedition had not been lively, but nee had never seen a place so subdued.

The checkpoint on the far side of town was larger than nee had anticipated, with heavy gates hewn from thick tree trunks. Their outer shell of bark had been left rough and unfinished, and Caran shuddered to imagine how ancient the trees must have been when they were slain to build the gates, anger surging through ner blood at the extravagant waste of such ancient beauty and power. Nee liked even less the look of the stationed soldiers: too many for so small a line, each heavily armed and armored. Three men patted down a traveler at the front of a short line, while a fourth held a menacing sword at the ready.

Misgiving curled in ner stomach, but Caran could not turn around. Nee had been seen, and there would be questions if nee were to balk at the gate. Nor were there better exits available to ner; the Eastborne wall extended for days in either direction, and every checkpoint would be the same as this one. Escape the way nee had come in, through the Mossmerrow swamp, was impossible because of ner journals; the delicate paper would be soaked in the crossing and the entire expedition would be wasted.

The only way out was through. Nee took a deep breath and stepped into line to be processed. The soldiers searching the poor soul at the front of the line liberated a small knife, three coins, and a packet of dried meat and chokeberries—the local travel ration. Caran kept ner face straight, but felt a measure of relief; nee had a small purse for them to plunder if the soldiers were only interested in thieving. Ner journals and pack of samples were the real treasures nee carried, and they were of value solely to Caran and ner sponsors.

Three more travelers were taken in turn and ner confidence grew. The soldiers were efficient in their greed but not cruel; belongings which had no worth to them were not destroyed in a show of bullying. Each victim was released after a thorough search, trudging out of Northnesse poorer for their trouble but free. Caran rehearsed in ner head how best to react when the soldiers inevitably divested ner of the few pieces of gold nee had retained. Alarmed but not angry, nee decided; upset, yet not in a threatening way.

Ner turn came. Caran stepped forward, boots clunking against the wooden platform. Nee set ner bags on the ground and spread ner arms wide in preparation for being searched. If they peeled up ner sleeves, they would not be able to read the tattoos there; if they patted through ner short razor-cut hair, they would snag their fingers but find nothing of value.

The invasive search would be unpleasant and unsettling but would be over quickly and nee would be on ner way, safe at last and knowing that ner sponsors would be overjoyed.

Soldiers moved forward with outstretched hands, then one of them checked his step in surprise. He gasped and shot a finger out, pointing to something above Caran's head. Ner heart sank as nee followed his gaze. Thick tree trunks formed rafters overhead, weeping with ancient power cut off in its prime. Nestled in their branches lay a gem the size of a man's eye. Caran had not noticed the jewel before but was quite sure that it had not been throbbing with an incandescent blue glow until after nee stepped forward.

Anyone with magical ability knew how dangerous it was to attempt travel through Northnesse since the witch-queen's rise to power, but it had not always been so. For generations, the witch-kings of the northern lands had welcomed the magically-inclined to their court, carving out places in their palaces for even the lowliest conjurer. Their advisors were solemn wizards and experienced hedge-witches; their queens and consorts were chosen from among the most powerful magi and enchantresses in all the five kingdoms.

Northnesse was renowned throughout the magical community as a place where mages of common birth could rise to the level of a prince if they were clever enough to master politics along with their craft. Yet not every witch and wizard in the five kingdoms was eager to emigrate there. Rumors spread of hidden dangers and unsavory practices among the gentry; things like necromantic divination were fine as far as they went, but lurid tales of necrurgists raising the bodies of dead laborers sounded a step too far. Whispers of powerful rivalries at court were another deterrent, causing many to hesitate before throwing their hat into the political ring.

Generations of in-fighting ravaged the noble ranks through private wars, infertility curses, and lethal 'accidents'. Fewer and fewer magi from neighboring kingdoms were willing to enter a political free-for-all to infuse fresh blood into an ailing aristocracy. When a young witch-queen ascended the throne as the last child of her dying line, people hoped for a turning point. Youth could rise from the ashes and the kingdom be reborn. All that was needed was the right witch or wizard to take the young queen in hand: guide her, bed her, and plant within her enough children to revive the monarchy.

Mages who had avoided the tumultuous kingdom were now moved to visit the court, drawn by tales of a reclusive young woman and imagining her to be easily mastered. Yet the docile girl the suitors were expecting turned out to be a willful queen in no mood to yoke herself in matrimony. One by one her suitors disappeared, dropping from public view so abruptly that they might as well have turned invisible. The kingdoms of their birth watched these events from a wary distance, uncertain whether to file official complaints through their ambassadors. Meddling in the affairs of witches was not an endeavor to undertake lightly.

More worrisome to the people of Northnesse were the draconian laws implemented by their young queen. The borders were closed, ending free travel and cutting families off from relatives in neighboring kingdoms. Injunctions were placed against the practice of magic anywhere in the land, and practitioners were ordered to report to the queen for royal examination. Hundreds of hedge-witches and palm-readers made their way to court in compliance with the law. None was seen or heard from again.

An exodus began. When the first wave of practitioners summoned to court failed to return, their spouses, children, and pupils gathered their belongings and ran. The first incarnation of the Eastborne wall was put up in a desperate attempt to stem the outward flow of bodies and goods to a more manageable trickle. A sprawling makeshift fence of stone and mud was patrolled by the royal army which had swelled its ranks overnight, paid from the coffers of those who had vanished.

Magic users who could not flee were taken in cages to the queen's court. Mages skilled in slipping bindings or sliding through bars were pierced with steel blades and iron arrows. More often than not, however, the captured were powerless to attempt escape. Cage bars did not bend at the caress of a seer's cards, nor would they melt away from a brush of an herbalist's sage. The most potent witches of the previous generations had belonged to noble lines which destroyed themselves in petty arguments; those who remained among the peasantry were dabblers and dilettantes, helpless to resist when soldiers came.

Roads were soon clogged with horse-drawn wagons bearing prisoners for the queen. Dissenters among the common folk were hanged and displayed from castle walls, while magi disappeared into dungeons. Unease swept the land like a pelting summer storm, bringing destruction in its wake. Books of magic were burned to prevent the teaching of new wizards, and any child born with magical talent was seized from their parents.

Towns learned to hide their healers and pregnant people when magic hunters came through, and clung to the cold comfort that these hunters were few and far between. Only those with magic could identify others blessed with the gift, and the queen did not suffer more than a dozen magicians to live in her land. Avoiding an accusation of magic in Northnesse was as simple as avoiding any and all who wielded it, or so Caran had thought until nee was betrayed by the glowing jewel set in the Eastborne gate.

The Northnesse purge was observed by the other four kingdoms with varying degrees of wary interest. None wished to invade their large neighbor to the north, and few rulers were above exploiting the purge. Refugees could be accepted in exchange for wealth and labor, and more than one court picked up new wizards, alchemists, and healers in service to the crown. In that sense, the cleansing of Northnesse had been a political boon for its neighbors, if the cost of human misery went uncounted.

In the space of a few months, however, the study and practice of magic was completely altered as Northnesse carved a brutal gash into the academic map. Whole disciplines were impacted by the closed borders: herbalists were denied access to native flora, oracles could no longer study fauna and their precious entrails, and every altar in the land was bereft of candles dyed in the colors of the northern flowers.

These goods and services could be replicated in time, but the flow of information which had continued uninterrupted for centuries, the study and observation of northern climes and the unique habitats therein, was irreplaceable to the magic community. Magic was a complex system that flowed around and through all things. Careful manipulation of any single part required an understanding of the whole, and the abrupt loss of Northnesse created a tremor that rippled out and disrupted myriad spells beyond its borders.

The Magic Guild could not allow this situation to continue. Waiting was not an option when a witch's longevity could be magically extended and the queen had come to her throne at a young age. Yet war was politically impossible when no ruler could be found willing to invade the northern giant on the urging of a few flustered academics, even if they were backed by those mages who used their powers in more martial disciplines. With few remaining alternatives, an approach of a stealthier bent was architected.

A series of infiltrations were devised, of which the first was the most important. An agent would slip into the kingdom and identify the best routes in and out, while gathering samples and sketches of native flora most vital to the magical arts. This agent would be selected from among the guild members who fitted necessary criteria: the ability to live on the road for several months; to pass as a local when visiting towns for supplies; and to keep their mouth shut if captured, as future expeditions would be endangered were the witch-queen to learn what was afoot. The agent should also be someone whose loss would not damage the community should they die; a simple conjurer was less valuable to the guild than a powerful wizard.

Caran was a hedge-witch with only minor herbal magic and no real importance within the guild, despite being a member in good standing. Nee had an undeniable talent for observation and record-keeping, with the ability to draw any plant in perfect detail and record in six different languages the habits of an animal. One of those languages was an alphabet of ner own devising, very unlikely to be deciphered in case of capture. Nee had lived on the road as a wandering healer for years before settling down in a small home in the eastern town of Freyhurst, and was well prepared for the rigors of the journey.

When Caran named a fee calculated to steal the listener's breath away, the guild grudgingly agreed. Price was little object when the information to be retrieved was invaluable. Over the coming weeks, an expedition was beautifully outfitted: the finest mule money could obtain, food preserved against all forms of rot, underclothes woven with enchantments to keep the wearer comfortable in any weather, and Northnesse coins bought from refugees at twice their face value so that Caran would not be carrying foreign currency.

While supplies were assembled, Caran meticulously charted ner route through the northern domain. Nee would enter through the Mossmerrow, a blighted swamp where knobby trees grew in knee-high water the color of a dying man's phlegm. All available maps had been created years before the border closings and were woefully out of date, but Caran judged ner trip through the swamp would take several days. The slog would be dangerous but if nee avoided reptiles, leeches, and moss-gnat swarms, nee would survive.

On crossing the swamp, nee would scatter what remained of ner supplies to the wild beasts and stop in the town of Stynston to purchase fresh food, clothes, and paper. Caran could not risk discovery by carrying foreign foods or wearing southern outerwear any longer than necessary; even the most careful spy could be undone by an errant hue of dye or woven patterns unique to another region. Nee would pretend to be a local traveling peddler of cures; not *magical* cures, of course, but the mundane tinctures and teas that were the only source of healing left to the good Northnesse people in the wake of their queen's terrible laws.

Depending on what nee learned in town, nee would move further north along one of several likely routes nee had mapped out. The easiest way to cross the Bluemere was by ferry, then Caran could turn east on the lonely winding road through the Winterwald, a forest whose white needles covered the track like a blanket of snow and where grew at least eighteen plants and flowers unique to the region. Ner journals were large and aching to be filled, as was the sack slung over ner mule for collecting samples.

Everything had gone more or less to plan, though a few unpleasant nights were spent dodging royal patrols before Caran learned to avoid the roads entirely. Nee had found samples aplenty and taken numerous specimens. Ner journals were filled with drawings of unfamiliar plants and animals, along with notes in ner private language detailing the condition of the roads, the locations of towns, the state of the weather, and landmarks to help ner craft a new map of the land for the guild on ner return. The most important of these details nee tattooed on ner arms and legs as nee rested by the campfire in the evenings, surrounding ner words with designs which pleased ner. Even if the precious paper notes were lost, nee wore ner experiences on ner skin.

The mule had been sold to a kindly farmer on ner way to Silvercrest and the Eastborne wall. Nee no longer had use for it and the guards at the gate would ask questions about the animal. The dried samples in ner bag were light enough to carry on ner back, along with the remaining rations nee would consume before the expedition was complete. When the farmer asked what name the mule answered to, Caran hesitated and gave him ner own. Nee liked to think ner name would live on even if nee did not.

The wooden bed of the prison wagon had been painted an imposing black, but the paint was flaking off to show a shabby beige underneath. Northern ash, Caran noted with dull interest as nee picked at the flaking splinters with ner fingernails. The wood was long dead, but even if a spark of lingering life had remained, nee was no druid; trees did not warp to ner will. Ner magic was of the subtle variety, just strong enough to feel the thrum of power in the metal bars forming the walls and ceiling of ner cage.

This wagon had been constructed to transport magic users, so nee supposed it made sense to layer the cage with spells to hold its prisoners. Yet Caran hadn't the training to tell what those spells were, what might trigger them, or how to dispel them. Nee was and always had been nothing more than an expendable hedge-witch. Competent enough to get by but nothing like the men and women conjured in public imagination by the word 'witch'. Nee grew herbs and collected the secrets of plants, cataloging that which would heal and that which would harm; valuable work that saved lives, but never flashy.

Trying to ignore the rattle of the wagon on the uneven road, Caran leaned back against the bars and took stock of ner situation. Nee was a magic user in a land which executed magic users; nee was also a spy, which was rarely good for one's health. Ner guild employers had warned Caran not to expect rescue or ransom, but even if they had promised intervention nee knew no way to convey a message to them. Before setting out, they had given ner a vial of poison to consume in case of capture but Caran had thrown it into the swamp with the rest of ner foreign supplies. Nee was on ner own with only ner wits.

Nee could throw nerself on the mercy of the witch-queen, but that plan hinged on her having any to spare: a prospect that seemed unlikely, given the brutality of the purges. Nor was nee enamored of the idea of working for the witch-queen in any capacity, when such a position would almost certainly involve tracking other magical prisoners and hauling them in identical cages to their deaths. Caran prided nerself on ner flexible

31

morality but nee drew a hard line at murder, which meant bargains of that sort were off the table.

If the witch-queen could not be negotiated with, perhaps her subjects might be more reasonable. Caran eyed the soldiers surrounding the wagon. They rode their horses as far from the cage as they could, never making eye contact or acknowledging its occupant in any way. They spoke in whispers, their quiet voices too soft to make out. This wasn't steely discipline, nee decided; fear was what hunched their shoulders and kept them out of ner reach. Were they so cowed by magic that they drew no difference between a witch-queen and a mere hedge-witch? Perhaps to the common folk of Northnesse there was none; to them, ner powers marked ner for either great privilege or painful death, depending on the whim of their queen.

Escape was impossible, mercy was dubious, and negotiation was improbable. Mundane options exhausted, nee turned reluctantly to magic for alternatives. The wagon rode low enough to the ground for Caran to stretch ner arms and brush the high grass lining the dirt road. Nee let ner fingers trail, watching the soldiers avoid looking at ner. They had taken ner sack of flora samples but ner clothes still had pockets. Options were limited by the availability of what pickings lay between here and their destination.

The local grass was lovely, long and high, brushing ner dangling hands as the wagon bumped along the country track. Farmers did not care for the grass, as it was a creeper whose roots spread underground and choked their crops; but those roots were wholesome food for cattle and horses, and dogs chewed the rough leaves to improve their digestion. Children gnawed on the roots as well, liking their sweet taste, and in times of famine the grass could be dried, ground into meal, and turned into bread. When the grass was cut and gathered, the long flexible leaves could be used to weave the stalks into baskets.

Neither bread nor baskets could help Caran now. Ner eyes searched the tall grass for spots of color nestled within the growth, the tools of ner craft. Stalks of dove's feet shot above the fray, their fuzzy red fronds unfurling to the noon sun; the furry weed was good for coughing fits and kidney pains when mixed with wine, but would not bend prison bars. Stringy white crone's hair waved in the wind as the wagon rolled past, but a tonic for period cramps would not aid Caran's escape. Fat leaves of adder's tongue caressed ner hands, but though their juice could cure breast ailments, bowel obstructions, sore eyes, bleeding noses, and sorrowful temperaments, they could not stop wagon wheels nor suborn soldiers to ner will.

Slumping lower against the bars, Caran scowled and closed ner eyes against the late afternoon sun. Ner search was a foolish grasp for hope, like the wild bargaining of condemned men as they were dragged to the gallows. Plants were beautiful, useful, wonderful things, but escape was not going to leap into ner fingers as the wagon trundled along. Caran was stuck here and the sooner nee accepted that truth the better.

Caran winced as the wagon rattled to a halt. One of the soldiers, a tall one whose armor was in better condition than that of the others, nudged her horse over to the cage. Nee waited, slouched against the bars, fingers still dangling in the grass. "The river ahead is the last before we reach Erivale castle," barked the woman, her eyes unreadable behind the long nosepiece and cheek-guards of her helmet. "We're stopping to water the horses. You will be fed, and we'll pass in buckets for you to wash and relieve yourself. Understand?"

This was more courtesy than Caran had expected as a prisoner being led to almost certain death. The soldier's tone was brusque but not cruel. Struggling to sit up nee decided to risk a request, hoping for no worse outcome than a stern denial. "May I leave the cage and walk down to the river instead? You've shackled my ankles so I can't run, and I'm no threat to you." This was true; if Caran had possessed enough magic to thwart ner captors, nee would have used it when they first laid hands on ner.

Eyes shielded by metal and shadow stared at ner while nee fought the urge to scratch at the fresh tattoos on ner arms. Caran didn't think of nerself as particularly fearful—nee had accepted this mission knowing the risks involved, after all—but after months spent free on the road, being caged was a misery. Nee recalled finding a fox gnawing at his own leg to escape a hunter's trap; Caran had freed the poor beast, not realizing at the time just how much nee shared in common with the animal.

"If you try to run, if you try *anything*," ner jailer warned, her voice stern and cold, "my archers will fill you so full of arrows you'll look like a tailor's pincushion. You hear me?"

"I understand." Caran nodded, keeping ner head meek and low as the woman rattled keys against the heavy metal lock and swung open the door. Nee pulled nerself up and stepped slowly to the wagon's edge, ner movements hobbled by the chains on ner feet.

"Faster, witch. We're not spending the night out here. Castle by high-moon, and I don't need you slowing us down with dawdling." Thick muscular arms reached up to help ner down, the tanned leather of the woman's gloves light against Caran's darker skin. Her touch was like her tone: tough but not unkind.

Caran swayed on ner feet, finding ner balance after the roll of the rattling wagon. "Thank you." Pausing as the woman waited impatiently nee started in the direction of the river, ner captor a few steps behind ner. "Do you have a name?"

"I do. No need for a witch to know it."

The rebuke was mild enough for ner to feel safe giving a soft laugh. "Well, while I am a witch, I'm just about the weakest witch you're likely to meet. I couldn't work magic with your name even if I wanted to." Nee cast a sidelong glance at the imposing woman, grateful that at least one member of the guard wasn't too cowed to speak with ner. "You don't need to be afraid of me, is what I'm getting at."

"Never said I was afraid," the woman pointed out, tone unchanged.

"By Northnesse law, a witch is a witch. You're either one of the queen's chosen or you'll be dead by dawn. Either way, no need to know my name."

"Chosen... hunters?" Caran hazarded, picking ner way more carefully where the ground turned soft and wet near the riverbank. Nee had been able to avoid magic hunters on the road, partly because there were so few of them, but every town had tales of the men and women who stole healers from their beds.

"Aye." The woman gave a brisk nod. "And designated successors until the queen bears a child of her own. Or so we're told; she cycles through her favorites and we bow to her will in all things."

Caran blinked at this piece of information, surprised to have it so freely given and in such an insubordinate manner. "I see. And if I should be one of these lucky chosen?" nee asked the brusque woman, tilting ner head with curious interest. "Would I know your name then?"

"No."

"Why not?"

The woman's reply was as cold as the northern wind. "In that case we wouldn't be friends, witch."

"I see." They had reached the riverbank and Caran knelt in the mud to cup ner hands with water and splash ner face. "You aren't afraid I'll repeat any of this, are you?" nee observed, looking back and up at ner jailer.

The woman, whose armor was in much better condition and more expensive than that of her peers, snorted at the question. "There are reasons why I'm assigned to the ass-end of the Eastborne wall, witch. Now drink up and wash yourself while I tend my horse. Remember, dive into that river and my archers will make sure you never come up for air."

Caran watched her stalk away, the setting sun glinting from the woman's armor and striking ner in the face with as much force as the words. Nee had encountered bluster in taverns on the road, but more often than not copious quantities of wine had been required to provoke such candor. Sober talk such as that required power behind it to keep the speaker alive, and armor like hers suggested wealth also.

In any other kingdom Caran would have set her down as disgraced nobility, the minor sort who were too much trouble to kill and useful to keep alive if they pledged their skills in service to the crown. Here in Northnesse, however, nobility was determined by magical talent. Ner jailer had none, Caran was certain; even if ner senses lied, the woman would have been caught in the purges. Without a trace of magic, she could never be noble; unless, Caran realized with a sharp breath, she was a child of mages and born without talent. They were rare, these magicless babies, but they did exist. A noble child lacking magic might well have escaped the purge but kept their heritage, if they were lucky.

Caran felt a stab of pity for the woman, even as nee knew ner feelings stemmed in part from a need for distraction from ner own dire situation. Nee sighed and bent to drink from the river, letting ner gaze sweep the bank where nee knelt. A wealth of reeds and flowers blossomed beside the life-giving water, but the specimens which met ner eyes were valuable only for forage or healing, or crafting into bedding or baskets or paper; no miracles sprang from the ground into ner hands.

Dejected, nee turned to stand and hobble back to the cage. Yet nee was distracted by a profusion of bright yellow flowers drinking in the last rays of the sun: maiden's joy, they were called back home. Caran used to bundle them into posies in the spring and sell them to lovers eager for pretty tokens to give their beloveds. Then nee frowned. It was late autumn edging into winter, and even if the season had been right the locale was not; maiden's joy was a southern plant which craved warmth above all else.

Three archers glared at ner back, arrows at the ready. Nee shuffled ner knees closer to the water and hunched ner shoulders forward to shield ner hands from prying eyes. With the utmost care, a murmured prayer to the southern goddess and her consort, and as much magic as nee could muster, nee pinched a stem with ner fingernails. Thick white pus oozed out and a slow stunned smile spread over Caran's face.

Quick as a flash nee went to work, plucking the stems and stuffing them in the pockets of ner cloak, murmuring charms to preserve the plants and prevent their sap from spilling out. Clearly, miracles *did* spring into needy hands for here, blooming in the orange dusk by the banks of the river, grew a rich profusion of king's favor.

They reached Erivale castle as the moon climbed over the high stone walls. Caran pulled ner cloak tighter around nerself as the wagon rattled over the drawbridge and passed under the largest barbican nee had ever seen. Two towers stood on either side of the fortified gatehouse, and soldiers peered at ner with a mix of fear and fascination in their eyes. Nee heard whispers of "*Witch!*" and "*A real one!*" as tiny blue gems studded in the stone walls and cobblestone path glowed in ner wake like the train of a wedding gown.

The night was cool, for which Caran was grateful; nee had an excuse to clutch at ner cloak and prevent the precious cuttings of king's favor from shaking out of the lined pouches sewn in ner clothes. Chilly breezes promising a bitter winter stirred fields of fat grains growing just outside the massive stone walls. These would soon be harvested and stored, feeding the castle inhabitants throughout the long winter. If provisions ran low the queen would presumably move her court to another castle and feed off the denizens there. Caran knew of at least three large castles within the Northnesse borders, and an untold number of noble country estates which had passed to the rapacious crown.

It was a shame, Caran reflected, that the young queen had inherited so much only to burn it all to the ground. A system of monarchy and nobility based on magic had drawbacks; the constant bickering and maneuvering for power had blighted the land. On a more personal level it had harmed people like ner jailer who were considered unfit to rule through an accident of birth, despite qualifications otherwise. Yet magic built these high stone walls, this towering barbican, and the imposing keep which held court at the center. Mages had fertilized the surrounding fields, instilling in them the power to produce fat bounty untroubled by weeds and pests. Without magical healing and plentiful food, many would suffer and the weakest would die.

The wagon rattled to a halt in the shadow of the keep, the moon blotted from the sky by the vast structure. Ner jailer dismounted from her horse, tossing the reins without a second glance to the sleepy-eyed stableboy who promptly appeared at her side. "On your feet, witch."

Caran struggled up and shuffled to the door. Ner jailer stooped over ner feet and nee heard the scraping of a key against iron before ner manacles fell away, clattering to the cage floor. The armored woman reached in to lift ner down to the ground. "Come on, down you go. You're not as light as you look, are you? Makes you wonder what witches eat."

"Small children," Caran deadpanned, finding ner balance in the darkness with the help of ner captor. Nee looked up into her face, wishing the moonlight were strong enough to see her eyes. "Aren't you afraid of me, or worried I'll run off? It'd be a shame to lose your prisoner so close to your destination."

The woman gave Caran a light shove on the shoulder to get ner moving. "Into the keep and mind the stairs. We're going up. Should I be worried, witch? You said yourself you were the weakest witch I would ever meet. Anyway," she added in a grim tone, "you're in the queen's territory now. If you're strong enough to escape her keep, no chain would hold you and no guard could keep you against your will. Myself included."

Caran nodded, feeling ner way up the stairs. Torches were set into the stone walls, but they were more likely to blind anyone who looked directly at them than to cast light. A shiver ran down ner spine, unrelated to the cold autumn air; deep magic filled this castle, laced with death. "May I ask what will be done to me?"

"I told you." Her voice was low behind Caran, a quiet murmur in the darkness. "You will be chosen by the queen or you will die."

38

Ner bowels felt watery and nee wondered for a useless moment if nee would be allowed to use a latrine before execution, but shook the thought away. "Were your parents chosen, or did they die too?"

A soft hiss in the dark. "What did you say?"

"Your parents." Caran kept climbing, going as slowly as nee could. "They were mages, were they not? I saw your armor—"

"My father was a healer," the woman cut in, her tone sharp and angry. "My mother was a princess, cousin to the queen. They met on the battlefield and married soon after. How they died is none of your concern."

"I'm sorry," nee told her, stinging at the rebuke. It was true that Caran was prying, but even a hint of what to expect at the top of these stairs was priceless to ner. "Please forgive me. Fear made me speak out of turn. If I must meet a princess of the royal blood in this castle, I would far prefer it to be you."

The soldier's voice was no warmer than before, but there was a hint of sour amusement. "I'm a lady by birth and nothing more. If anyone here has a claim to royal titles it would be you, oh weakest of witches. If I don't like the fact that my talentless blood means I rank lower than a foreign-born spy who can barely cast a cantrip, I can comfort myself at night with the fact that I'm alive. That's worth all the glowing blue gems in the crown jewels to me."

"Ever thought of emigrating?" Caran tried to match her dry tone. "There are folk in neighboring kingdoms who would see your worth; it's hard to miss, in fact."

"Are you offering to run away with me, little witch? I don't see that working out well for either of us."

"I, uh, wouldn't mind trying. Better than the alternative awaiting me upstairs."

She laughed, but there was no mirth in the sound. "True enough. But this is my home. We're here."

Caran didn't understand what she meant with those last two words

39

until ner foot lifted automatically for the next step and found only empty air. Nee would have sprawled forward but for the steadying hands of ner guard. Torches partly illuminated the wide landing they stood upon and the heavy iron doors that led to ner fate. Nee took a hesitant step forward and then looked back.

"If I don't ever see you again, my name is— *was* Caran."

Shadows danced over the face of ner escort, her thoughts impossible to guess. "Janeida, little witch," she said, taking up a stance by the wall to wait. "Lady Janeida. Farewell."

The closest nee had been to a throne room was the Magic Guild's receiving hall in Linlea. Leaders of the guild had met with Caran prior to ner expedition, sitting around a low circular table in a brightly-lit hallway which led off into rooms on either side, each filled to the ceiling with books arranged by category of study. Nee had not felt entirely at home in the scholarly place, but it had a peacefulness nee could not deny.

In contrast, the throne room in Erivale castle was dark and imposingly vast. Thick carpet marked a path from the iron doors to a dais at the other end of the hall, where two thrones inlaid with gold and glowing blue jewels glittered in the light of braziers ringed about the raised platform. The place must have been built with sorcerers in mind, for in addition to the fire-pans ringing the dais, two streams of water flowed in gutters on either side of the carpet path, air rushed in from windows nee could not see and made the flames dance, and rectangular columns of earthen bricks added the fourth natural element to the room.

It felt wrong. The sides of the room disappeared into shadow, untouched by the flickering light and making Caran feel claustrophobic and choked despite the size of the room. The numerous braziers made the room too hot even as the cold northern wind bit into ner flesh. Through and over and under it all was the thrum of death and old magic, the feeling of a place where too much badness has happened over too long a time.

"Welcome. Come in, come in. Closer." The voice was light, almost cheerful. A young woman lounged in one of the golden thrones, her eyes fixed on Caran with intense scrutiny. "It has been a long time since I've had to conduct such an interview. The last one they brought me was months ago and that was a false alarm, more charlatan than fortune-teller. But I've seen how you light up my little gems. Do come closer."

Caran stepped reluctantly onto the carpet path, feeling the blast of heat as nee approached the braziers. A fleeting fantasy of tipping over the flame-pans and burning the castle to the ground tempted ner, but the witch-queen of Northnesse could surely bend flame to her will, especially when her throne room was fitted to the needs of an elemental sorceress. Who else could benefit from the earth, fire, water, and air in the room when every other sorcerer in the kingdom had been put to death in the purge?

"Your majesty is too kind to greet me," Caran managed to utter, ner voice dry against the heat. "I was apprehended by your soldiers in Silvercrest. I only wished to sell my herbal teas on the other side—"

Laughter cut ner off, a tinkling giggle like ringing a string of bells. "Please spare me such fictions. You are a spy, my dear; though I don't know who sent you. Would you like to tell me?" Bright eyes flashed in the firelight. "Not that I particularly care, I confess. I don't even mind if they send more, so long as they're one at a time like this. Very accommodating of your masters. You *are* alone, aren't you?"

Caran blinked at the woman, surprised to hear a discordant note in the question. "Yes, I am alone, Your Majesty." This would have been ner answer even if nee *did* have a partner; nee had no interest in confessing names on a torture rack.

The queen seemed to read the same conclusion in Caran's face, her eyes narrowing with suspicion. "I don't know that I believe you; all the more reason not to dally."

Nee braced nerself for the call, a shout for the guards to come and drag the prisoner away. Instead the queen leaned back in her seat and tilted her head, studying Caran with a wisp of a smile on her face. Nee waited, confused, and then choked as cold air shot between ner teeth and thrust down into ner lungs. The sensation was like water when drunk wrong, the heaving coughing sensation of liquid where none should be. Yet it was *air*, icy and merciless, squeezing the life from ner chest. Nee reeled and slammed into an earthen pillar, hand snaking up the rough sun-dried brick in search of an anchor to steady nerself.

"Tell me," said the queen, her voice mild and curious, "do they have magic thieves in your part of the world? We're mages of a sort but, instead of doing magic of our own, we steal the magic of others." She giggled again, rolling her shoulders in a shrug. "Of course, I'm almost everything now: witch, wizard, magus, sorceress, enchantress. You name it, I've eaten it, but I started life as a thief."

The queen was too far to reach but Caran stumbled towards her anyway, one hand clutching at ner throat while the other clawed at ner cloak in a panic. Nee had thought to be more composed in the face of death, but faced with the loss of all air there was only raw fear and clumsy movements. The queen watched ner approach without alarm, head tilted again as she studied Caran's lurching steps with a detached manner.

"We're put to death in Northnesse," she mused. "It's the law. Can't have thieves running around stealing a king's power, can you? It happens in other places too, though I hear elsewhere it's by private assassination rather than public execution. But my mother and father were king and queen, and they hid me away; kept me safe until I could assume the throne." A shadow of a smile flitted over her face. "I'm afraid I may have sped that part up, but I had to. They thought we should tell the people what I am, and risk the danger. I disagreed. You'd have done the same in my place; anyone would."

Caran's head jerked from side to side, but not in denial. Nee sought fire in a room which was growing increasingly dark to ner eyes. Yet if nee couldn't see the fire, nee could seek out its heat; Caran reached out ner hand as nee stumbled forward.

"You don't think you would?" The queen was still talking, almost to herself, her words an indecipherable babble in Caran's ringing ears. "I think you're lying again. You see, a prophet swore at my birth that I would be killed by another mage—*two* mages, to be precise—and I intend not to be killed at all. So, while I was very grateful to my mother and father, I couldn't take the risk. What are you doing?"

Heat. The edge of the metal brazier burned Caran's hand, but nee was past caring. Nee yanked handfuls of king's favor from the folds of ner cloak, trusting to ner herbal charms to keep the sap contained in the stalks rather than seeping into ner skin. Caran thrust the lot into the fire and kept ner fingers there until nee was certain the blossoms were aflame. "What *is* that? It smells foul—!"

A battery of choking coughs echoed through the chamber, but this time the rasping rattle for breath did not come from Caran. As suddenly as a bucket of water splashed over a dreamer's face, the queen's spell was broken; ner sight was sharp as a blade just in time to witness a cloud of white smoke spreading out into the room from the burning coals. With the last of ner strength, Caran grasped the searing edges of the pan and pushed the brazier over onto the dais, coals scattering around the queen's feet and the white smoke billowing up to envelop her.

Caran dove to the floor, gasping for the last pocket of clean air while nee shoved the edges of ner cloak into the little water gutter nearby. Thirsty wool drank deeply and Caran stretched the wet cloth over ner nose and mouth, gobbling lungfuls of breath through the makeshift filter. When nee looked up, the witch-queen knelt among the burning embers, doubled over and retching. Between hacking coughs, her words spat at Caran as nee scrambled back from the dais. "What... did... you do?"

A real herbalist would know or strongly suspect what poison was in her system, based on the orange hue, the shape of the blossom, and the deadly white pus that vaporized into smoke when it touched flame. When the witch-queen absorbed the power of the Northnesse herbalists, she must not have taken their knowledge. Nee would not rectify that now, deeming silence the wisest response. Caran's own charms would protect ner as long as nee did not stray any closer to the deadly fog.

Ignoring the pain in ner hands, nee struggled to ner feet and moved backwards into the shadows to wait. The queen's clouding eyes followed ner movements as she collapsed to the floor. "You can't kill me," she rasped. The coughing fit had passed but blood dribbled from the edges of her lips. "The seer swore I would be killed by both man and woman working in unison, two witches ending my life with magic. You're just one spy."

Caran considered pity, but the scratch in ner throat was too raw. "I am one spy, Your Majesty. I'm also both man and woman. I have been so since birth, and my magic allowed me to handle the plant that is now killing you." Nee sighed and shook ner head, feeling more tired than triumphant. "I never had any intention to harm you, until you captured me and forced my hand. You murdered thousands, only to be slain by a hedge-witch whose talents are just adequate to harvest poisonous plants. Was it worth it?"

Her answer, if she made one, was lost in a bloody gurgle. Caran waited until death was certain, then opened the iron doors and slipped out. Outside, Janeida started from where she'd been resting against the wall. "What happened?" she demanded, eyes wide as she took in Caran's sopping wet cloak clutched to ner nose.

"She's dead," Caran answered with no joy in the telling. "Don't go in there. The room won't be safe for anyone else until morning. Thank the stars she left the windows open, otherwise the poison would take days."

The woman's eyes almost leaped from her head. "*Poison?*"

Caran hesitated, realizing belatedly the danger nee was still in. "We call it 'king's favor'," nee offered, letting ner heavy cloak fall away from ner lips. "It's quite lethal without the necessary protective charms. Anyone who eats the sap or inhales the smoke when it burns will die without immediate treatment."

Janeida stared at ner and Caran could see the questions in her eyes. When she opened her mouth to speak after a deep breath, however, all she said in her gruff tone was, "Interesting name."

Nee choked back a laugh born of panic, grateful to be alive for a little longer. "Well, the southern herbalists have a morbid sense of humor. Lovely golden-orange blooms, as rich to look at as any other flower you could name; but it'll turn on you as soon as not and its wrath is lethal. So."

The woman shook her head in exasperation. "Yeah, little witch, I got the joke. Now what?"

Caran stared at her, licking ner cracked lips and longing for dry clothes against the lingering draft. "You could take me home?" nee suggested, lifting ner eyebrows in supplication and daring to dream.

Janeida nodded. "I could take you home," she agreed, her gaze direct in the flickering darkness. "I could take you to the Eastborne wall while people panic over the queen's death and her favorites backstab each other in a bid for power. Or you could stay in Northnesse where by law a witch is a witch, and every witch is a valid claimant to the throne regardless of the strength of their magic. I can tell you right here and now that every man, woman, and child in this keep would rather crown the weakest witch I'll ever meet than one of the dead queen's hunters." She held Caran's eyes with her own. "So now what?"

Nee blinked at her, feeling dizzy after the combination of cold and heat, of ner fear and subsequent relief. Ner hands ached where the fire had singed them, and nee longed to find the right herbs in ner sack of samples to heal them. Most of all, nee wanted a good night's sleep and possibly a guard to ensure nee wouldn't be choked to death in the night. The experience had left ner with no desire for a repetition.

"We need you, Caran." A note of desperation in Janeida's voice tugged at ner heart. "The hunters would continue the late queen's policy of killing their competition, but you could stop the purges. You could tear down the wall and bring back our healers and let babies grow up in peace without being taken from their parents on the say-so of a glowing gem. You could help us and we would help you."

"A crown *and* a promise not to stab me in the back as long as I don't turn horribly evil?" Caran sighed and sagged backwards against the iron door, running a hand over ner eyes. "You realize if I do this, the Magic Guild won't pay my wages?" nee pointed out, a dry smile finding its way into ner voice. "You'll be crowning an impoverished hedge-witch of no account within the Guild, with a shady past as a spy for hire."

Janeida flashed ner a triumphant smile, throwing a steadying arm around ner shoulders and shuffling ner down the stairs. "We'll have the royal accountants send them a bill, obviously. You have a lot to learn about nobility, don't you? We behave as though money means nothing to us, but in truth we're parsimonious to a fault. You're lucky you have me at your side to explain these things. Now let's clean you up, Your Majesty. You have an image to maintain, shady history notwithstanding."

HIS FATHER'S SON

Content Note: Violence and Sexualized Violence; Bloodshed;
Death of Family, Parents, and Minor Children

Steel rang against steel as Nocien's saber struck his master's blade. A dozen clear notes sang in quick succession, each marking another metal kiss while his feet danced over the smooth earth of the circle: step forward, step back, lunge in, leap out. Each step was a light bounce, always ready to reverse away from unexpected trouble or to press forward towards a glimpsed opportunity. The trick was to stay moving, never slowing down or pausing for breath. A tired opponent became sloppy, making mistakes and leaving openings for attack. Stamina as much as skill determined the outcome of any battle.

Master Hilon lunged forward with his blade and Nocien threw himself backwards as his wrist twisted, bringing his own sword around to parry. Another beautiful clang sang out as their swords met, accompanied by the soft scuff of dirt under his feet. The footwork was almost second nature to him now, as much a part of his body as the dances he'd been taught as a child by his mothers. He felt the urge to laugh, delight bubbling up through his throat, but he knew by now not to waste the breath. Every scrap of air, every speck of his attention, must be devoted to the fight or he would lose his head.

47

There! An opening, he was sure. Nocien lunged forward as Hilon stepped back from his parried attack, swinging his blade to strike his master's wrist; if he could take off the hand, or at least sever the wrist cords, his opponent would drop his sword and the battle would be won. His saber connected, slapping the hard leather glove that covered his master's hand and arm up to the elbow, but Hilon's blade twisted in the air; it caught and threw glittering sunlight as naked steel carved a wide cut across Nocien's unguarded chest.

"Hold!"

Nocien lowered his sword, panting for air; worked up as he was, his armor felt too tight and his protective mask too stifling. He was hot and sweaty and the muffled voice from behind his mask sounded belligerent even to himself. "I disarmed you, master! I struck true and hit your wrist before the cut."

Master Hilon shook his head and a few long strands of hair escaped their bindings under his helmet to trail on the breeze. "Your hit wouldn't have stopped my cut, Nocien. You slowed the strike but it was still deep enough to kill. You're dead now and have only mildly inconvenienced me for your trouble; my wrist will heal."

"Well, of course your wrist is only lightly wounded, Master; I was holding back!" Even with thick boiled leather covering their faces, arms, and chests, both fighters had to practice care when using real blades. Nocien had been allowed to hit harder while training on switches cut from trees, back when he was learning how to aim and channel force into each blow. Now that they were perfecting his balance and technique, he was forced to moderate his strikes and sessions tended to descend into argument.

Grave eyes studied Nocien from behind the opposing helmet. "So your plan was to hit hard enough to take off my hand before I could cut you, thus rendering the opening you left impossible for me to seize?"

Nocien chewed his lower lip, not liking the options laid out before him. He would have preferred to argue he'd left no opening at all, but

48

the leather covering his chest boasted a long pucker below his collarbone in proof to the contrary. Therefore, either the opening was an accident or he'd allowed it on purpose; one explanation was a blow to his pride but the other was false. He'd not *planned* to create an opening, he'd just seen an opportunity and leaped after it, overjoyed at the prospect of defeating his master—a rare treat in the ring.

"I thought I saw a chance to disarm you," he admitted, looking away to study one of the brush shrubs ringing the campsite. "My plan was to end the fight quickly with a decisive attack." He rallied, belligerence creeping back into his voice. "It was a strategy to avoid drawing out the fight in case of other attackers."

His master's laugh was little more than a huff of air. "Well, you certainly did end the fight quickly. Nocien, an attempt to disarm is good but not when it leaves you open to attack; you can't gamble on its success to save your life. And if you're expecting numerous opponents, risky attacks that leave you open to being wounded are even less wise than usual; you'll die from attrition." A pause ensued, almost gentle. "You know that."

Nocien was glad his face was hidden behind his mask, feeling heat rise under the birthmark on his cheek as he flushed. He *did* know better, but had been carried away in the pleasure of the fight and forgotten the reason for his training. He couldn't afford to learn careless habits just because these practice matches weren't real. Taking a deep breath, he hefted his saber. "Sorry, master. Start again?"

Hilon lifted his saber to touch Nocien's in midair. "Not yet. Swing at my wrist again, the way you did before but more slowly. There, stop and hold. You see how I twisted to exploit your opening?" He moved his blade in a wide arc, sweeping over Nocien's chest as gently as a feather. "Can you tell me how the same attack could be made without leaving you open to a counterattack?"

Sweat beaded on his forehead behind the mask and the urge to scratch became almost overwhelming. Nocien pushed aside the discomfort as best he could, studying the frozen scene and ignoring the ache in his stationary arm. If he stepped closer, he'd just bring his chest further into Hilon's blade; if he stepped back, he wouldn't be able to connect at the wrist in order to disarm him. "I need longer arms," he observed, shaking his head with old annoyance. His build was slighter than Hilon's, something no amount of training would alter.

"The battle doesn't go to the man with the longest arms," countered Hilon, laughing another soft huff. "Lean up on the balls of your feet. Support your weight with your toes and arch your shoulders back."

Nocien blinked at the command. "What?"

"Lean up on—"

He shook his head. "I *heard* you, master. I don't understand, but I'll try."

The order seemed preposterous, but Nocien took a breath and pushed so his heels lifted from the ground and only the front halves of his feet carried his weight. The blade pointing at his chest dipped lower on his body as he rose, and as he rolled his shoulders back he was able to draw away from the saber without losing his position at Master Hilon's wrist. He blinked and looked up at his master's waiting eyes.

"What have you learned, Nocien?"

"Flexibility can make up for my shorter arm length? But, master, I'm easily off-balanced when contorted like this." He wobbled in the warm summer breeze to demonstrate the effect. "I can't fight on my toes."

This earned a chuckle. "No. You can't fight on your toes. But you can land on your toes when you lunge for the disarm and pull your shoulders back when my wrist turns. Every finger-length away from a blade counts. You're already light on your feet, Nocien; lighter than any of my boys. You can be lighter still."

Nocien was glad again of the mask covering his face, this time because it hid the gratified smile that flickered over his lips before he caught it. Hilon brought his sword up to clink against the opposing saber in a starting salute. "Now we start again. Look for the same opening this time and attempt to disarm—"

"Father!"

The two men whirled as one, turning in the direction of the frantic shout. Lykos, the youngest of Hilon's sons, rode at full pelt on his horse towards their camp. The animal's hooves thundered against earth and Lykos lay low along its back, urging it on harder. Nocien tore off his protective mask and helmet, observing Master Hilon do the same as the boy charged into the fighting circle and brought his mount to a panting halt.

"Report." Hilon's voice was cool and steady, and he took the reins of the animal as Lykos swung down.

"Father, scouts on the northern ridge." Lykos doubled over, gasping for air, his hands gripping his knees. Hilon hurriedly handed the reins to one of his kinswomen so he could bring a water-skin to the boy. Nocien fought the urge to rush him, knowing that Lykos had trouble breathing under stress, but his heart beat harder than a drum. "Dust on the horizon and flashing steel inside."

"A kin on the move?" Hilon rubbed a gentle hand over the boy's back as he gulped water, but his face was grave; Nocien knew how many bad reasons and how few good ones there were for a kinship to approach theirs without advance warning from the autarch. Such warnings prevented lethal misunderstandings.

Nocien tasted blood and wondered when he'd bitten the inside of his lip. "What color was their flag?"

Lykos looked up from the water-skin, his eyes wide with fear. "Blood-red. Autarch Guyon and his kinship are coming."

"I want you to come with us."

The camp was in a controlled uproar. Guyon and his band of thugs would not reach the site for at least a day, but readying a few hundred kinsfolk and their animals to break camp and move in that short time took

51

tremendous effort. Nocien moved swiftly about his tent deciding what to pack, what to burn, and what to bury on the slim chance he might return this way alive.

"Nocien, did you hear me? I want you to ride with us."

Master Hilon stood inside the flap of his tent, watching him pack. Nocien knew he shouldn't be there at all; as autarch of the kinship, Hilon had more pressing matters to deal with than the placement of an orphan foundling. To argue with him now in the midst of this crisis would be the height of disrespect. Better to let him return to more important things, while Nocien gathered himself and plotted Guyon's death.

"I heard you, master. Thank you. Are there enough horses or do you want me in the wagons again?" The last time the kin broke camp, Nocien had been too badly wounded to sit in a saddle.

"There are enough horses to go round. Myrrhine and her father are riding in the wagons with the children."

Nocien nodded, not looking up from his packing. Myrrhine was the youngest daughter of Master Hilon's third wife, and both she and her father were absolute terrors with blades in their own right. Knowing Myrrhine, she wouldn't enjoy being placed with the children, but Nocien could think of no one better to protect the young ones than the hotheaded girl and her fair-tempered father.

"My sons and I will ride at the head of the kin," Hilon continued, his dark eyes following Nocien as he moved about the small tent gathering his things. "Nocien, I want you there with us at the front."

The offer, unexpected and unlooked-for, stole Nocien's breath away. Hilon was autarch of the kin because he was their best and brightest, and his sons carried their father's legacy proudly. No one doubted that one of his children would be elected autarch when the unthinkable occurred and Master Hilon breathed his last. For an orphan foundling to be counted among his own accomplished offspring was an extravagant gesture.

"You do me great honor, master," Nocien managed, his voice struggling not to crack. He kept his face averted, not wanting Master Hilon to see the tears he blinked away. "Thank you."

He could feel Master Hilon's concerned eyes on his back. "You have thanked me twice, Nocien, yet you have not accepted. Will you look at me and tell me you will be there, riding with us?"

Nocien faltered, the tunic he'd been gathering up slipping from his hands to crumple to the ground. He straightened to face his master, opened his mouth, and found himself unable to utter a word. He was physically capable of lying to Master Hilon, of forcing the sounds through his mouth and into the air between them, but hadn't the heart to do it.

"I can't." The words were a whisper laden with guilt. To reject so kind an offer was the deepest discourtesy Nocien could display to his host and master, but acceptance was impossible. "I *want* to. But I can't."

"You can," urged Hilon. He didn't attempt to cross the short distance between them, but Nocien could judge how much his master wanted to embrace him by the way his hands opened helplessly at his sides. "Nocien, everyone in the kinship accepts you as one of our own. You're a good hunter, an excellent scout, and a hard worker. You have a family here. Please stay with us."

Nocien shook his head, praying that his voice wouldn't betray him and break; if that happened, he knew he really would cry. "Master, to be offered a courtesy position in your family is a great kindness—"

"It is no courtesy!" Hilon reached for him, his hands gripping Nocien's shoulders with gentle strength. "You are as much my child as any whom my wives have given me to claim before our kin. If my word is not enough for you, we can make your entry into our family as formal as you desire. Pick any one of my sons to marry, Nocien; they all adore you and would leap at the chance to have you."

This offer was *not* new; Hilon had brought him similar offers in the past, though Nocien refused to be wed to any man. Yet he was almost grateful for the well-worn tread of the old argument to drive away the gathering storm of tears. Unless a miracle occurred, this would be the last time Nocien felt a fatherly touch, so though his frustration was keen he shook his head gently so as not to dislodge his master's hands from his shoulders. "Master Hilon, even if I were worthy of such honor, I don't wish to be a wife to anyone ever."

Hilon gazed down at him, his dark eyes grave. A dozen heartbeats passed between them, and he nodded as if making a decision. "Then be a husband," he said, his voice softer now. "Marry one of my daughters."

"Master?" Nocien blinked, stunned to hear this suggestion from Hilon's lips.

His master shook his head, sighing with rueful resignation. "You must know Xenia adores you. She hasn't the slightest interest in blades until you practice, then she drops whatever she's doing and comes running to watch. And I see the way Phile's eyes follow you since she nursed you back to health after we found you. Either would be happy as your wife. Or if you prefer a huntress to a healer, Myrrhine would fight for the honor. She is my wife's daughter and not my own, but you would be assured of your place here with us."

Nocien felt as short of breath as Lykos after a hard run. To say he hadn't imagined such possibilities would be a lie, but he had never pretended these options were open to him. He was an orphan and an outsider, limiting his value as a husband to the strength in his sword-arm or the skill in his plow hand. To rise from dust to the son-in-marriage of a kinship autarch and his own master was little more than a fond idea to be indulged whenever the girls brushed his hand or teasingly held his gaze over Master Hilon's dinner table.

"You would allow that, master?"

Hilon gave him a warm smile, the one Nocien associated with safety since glimpsing it so many times during those dangerous days when he was still slipping in and out of consciousness from his wounds. "I have considered you one of my own children since the day I found you bleeding

54

on the border of our hunting lands. Nocien, there are many things I do not understand. I confess I once thought to gain a daughter with you, but I would be just as blessed to count you as my son. Come with us."

Nothing in heaven or earth could tempt him so much as this. Nocien dashed tears from his eyes as he shook his head. "I want to say yes, master. I would like very much to be your son."

"Then leave with us," the older man urged. "Nothing is stopping you from saying yes but yourself."

"I swore an oath." Nocien couldn't meet those dark eyes, finding it easier to look away. "You know I did. How could I be worthy of you as my father if I broke my word to my first father, my birth father?"

Grave eyes studied him, the older man's brow knit with worry. "My son, I did not know your birth father, but I cannot think he would want you to throw your life away on a quest for vengeance. What I know of him through you leads me to believe he would want you to live happily with us. Or at the very least to train with us further before you leave! Guyon and his men will still be here once you are ready to face him."

Nocien shook his head again and gently disentangled himself from the embrace. "If I settle down, if I move with the kinship and marry, I'll lose my nerve. Master Hilon—no, *Father*—I have to go. You've healed me and trained me and I will forever owe you a debt. All I can offer is a promise that I will try to return."

Hilon sighed and ran a hand through his hair, accepting defeat. His words were a soft farewell in the dark tent. "Be safe, my son. If Guyon does not kill you, come and find the kin. We move east to the sea."

Nocien had sworn his oath two harvest seasons ago when the night breezes had turned cool and life seemed likely to go on in the same way it always had. He'd been on the cusp of adulthood, rapidly approaching the age when his childhood name would be shed so that he might choose a new one, and still slept in his mother's tent. He was asleep when Guyon and his men stormed the camp, bringing fire and death in their wake.

The tent was small, just big enough to cozily shelter the three of them: Rhonwen, third wife of Autarch Cadfen; Nocien, fifth of Cadfen's eight children and one of sixteen born by the autarch's five wives; and Tegwen, who took a wife's name when she came of age yet married no man, living instead with Rhonwen in her tent and dancing with her on festival nights when the moon shone full on her bare arms. Nocien slept apart from Rhonwen and Tegwen in a little area partitioned by curtains, a place of his own.

Nocien liked Tegwen; from birth he had called her 'Mother' just as he addressed Rhonwen, who had born him, and the rest of his father's wives. Children were precious within the kinship and each child had as many mothers as were needed to thrive. Nocien was blessed with six mothers, but some of his siblings had seven or eight or even a dozen to raise them. Fathers were different, of course; there was usually only one father. The mother who bore the child presented the infant to the father and he in turn presented the child to their kin, granting the infant their childhood name and a place within the kinship.

Tegwen was the one who woke him, shaking him awake while covering his mouth with her hand. Nocien swam to the surface of his dreams and broke through to the other side, wondering why he heard shouts and smelled fire. He could *see* fire, too; Tegwen was lit from behind by a red glow that accentuated the fair splotches on her tan face and hands. Her eyes were wide with fear, and she spoke in a whisper.

"Get up quickly and quietly. Men are attacking the camp; we must go."

Nocien rubbed blearily at his eyes and sat up, reaching for his boots. "I don't understand. What men? Where is Mother Rhonwen?" Canvas walls glowed against the fire outside, illuminating the two of them inside an otherwise empty tent. Rhonwen was gone and her boots were missing.

Tegwen shook her head, long brown hair spilling over her shoulders; she'd not had time to braid it, Nocien realized, and somehow this scared him more than the looming shouts and clash of metal outside. "Rhonwen took her spear to fight. You and I are going to the western spring. She will meet us there. Come!"

He frowned as he yanked on his boots. Rhonwen was the best huntress in the kin and could hold her own against any animal under the sun or moon, but men were not beasts. "Can't we help her?" Nocien wasn't allowed on big game hunts yet but had taken down smaller animals with the other young hunters.

"She'll fight better if she's not worried about us," Tegwen said, holding him in a firm grip by the upper arm.

Their tent had been pitched far from the center of the campsite, and chaos had not yet enveloped the back. Drawing him to the rear, Tegwen pulled a knife from her skirt and dragged the sharp cooking tool down the length of the canvas. The rip of the material rang loud in Nocien's ears, but was lost under the roar of fire, the clash of metal, and the screaming. "Come," insisted Tegwen, pulling him out into the semi-darkness.

A red-orange glow remained at their backs as they crept through the darkness, their eyes struggling to readjust after exposure to the firelight. Nocien kept his head down and gritted his teeth, trying to block out the sounds behind them. "Tegwen. Tegwen! Where is Father?"

Her whisper was so low he had to strain to hear her. "He's with the fighters, I'm sure. Rhonwen went to help him. They will try to repel the attackers while we get the children out. Now keep your voice down—"

A soft gasp ripped from her as a hand clamped around her throat. A shadow which had loomed like a tree now resolved into a man. He held her at arm's length and laughed as her fingers scrabbled against his grip. "Trying to escape? Are you one of Cadfen's women, pregnant with one of his whelps? We're supposed to run through the women in case they're carrying, but it seems like a waste of such a pretty face."

Tegwen's legs kicked as the man lifted her by the neck, her head lolling back as air was crushed from her. Nocien darted forward in the darkness, grabbed the knife from Tegwen's skirt, and drove it into the man's belly without pause for thought. The man gurgled in surprise as the blade dragged across him and life gushed out in a rapid waterfall, but Nocien blocked the sound from his ears; it was easier to concentrate on the roar of his own heartbeat and steadying Tegwen as the man crumpled to the ground.

His mother leaned against him in the darkness, choking as she gulped down all the air she'd been denied. "We have to… keep going," she coughed, tugging at Nocien's arm in the direction of the western spring.

"No." He shook his head and gripped the bloody knife with both hands. "*You* keep going; crouch low and run quiet. Go to the spring. I'll follow and meet you there." She seemed poised to argue, the pale splotches on her face stark in the dim starlight against the darker brown canvas of her skin, but he pressed on. "I *must* go back for Father and the other mothers. You heard him!"

A heartbeat passed in silence, then Tegwen gathered him up in her arms and kissed his forehead. "Go," she whispered, her voice hoarse but still strong. "Be brave and smart and safe. I will be waiting for you and Rhonwen at the spring." With a final look back, she fled into the darkness and he was alone.

Nocien took a deep breath and looked down at himself. He was wet and cold, his clothes stained black with the blood he'd spilled. Nocien had never killed a person before; never considered that he might. He thought that he should feel something, but there was only a numb emptiness. Shaking his head, he turned back to the camp, the light of the raging fire splashing over his face and making him squint with pain. He didn't know what he could do to save his family, but he had to try. Kicking off from the slick ground, he ran.

Nocien's eyes had adjusted to the firelight before he reached the campsite, but he almost wished they had not. More bodies lay on the ground, some partially covered by the canvas of collapsed tents and others charred from the fire that swept around the camp perimeter looking for fuel to devour. Some of the dead were strangers to him, but too many were men and women he knew; hunters and farmers of the kinship. One of the men he recognized as the father of three of Mother Ceinwen's children, and Nocien had to dash tears from his eyes and keep running. He couldn't help the dead, but he might be able to help the living.

The screams were less frequent now and farther away than before; though he still heard the clash of metal in the center of the camp, he imagined most of the kin had scattered into the night. He could hear their calls in the brush looking for their loved ones or, he fervently hoped, howling in fury as they killed their pursuers. Then a cry tore at his heart, a voice he knew as intimately as his own: his littlest sister Mabyn sobbing in a helpless rage.

He darted around a large tent still standing and pulled up short in shock. Rhonwen stood in the firelight bathed from brow to knee in blood. She clutched her spear in her left hand, leaning on the weapon as though it were a tent pole keeping her upright. On the ground around her lay bodies, the dead almost a dozen in number. Two mothers huddled nearby, sheltering in their arms three of Nocien's sisters.

A single strange man faced Rhonwen with an unfamiliar sword in his hands; not the short cutting implement the hunters used to hack away brush and tree limbs, but a thin weapon for stabbing. Longer than Rhonwen's spear, the sword was tipped with blood. The huntress' tunic was torn and stained with wounds. The man laughed and feinted at Rhonwen, mocking her sluggish dodge, tormenting her.

Even as the fires raged and screams drifted on the wind, Nocien felt a strange peace. The world slowed around him, and he stepped out of his body to watch himself move. The stranger had his back to him and

Nocien's feet closed the distance. He was shorter than the other man, but the cooking knife was long and easily stabbed up through the stranger's neck. If he gurgled, Nocien couldn't hear above the roar in his ears.

Arms swept around him. Branwen, the dark-haired mother who walked with a limp and always had a kind word for Nocien, wrapped him in a hug as the body lurched forward. Her hands shielded his eyes, which seemed odd to Nocien since he was the one who had caused the sight. He looked at Rhonwen and was glad to see her supported by Eurwen, the golden-skinned wife who spoke with her hands instead of her mouth. Eira, his oldest sister, held Mabyn in her arms while Tesni clung to Eira's sleeve and tried to look brave.

"Where is Tegwen?" Rhonwen's voice was hoarse with smoke and blood as she leaned heavily on her spear. "She was supposed to be with you."

Nocien shook his head, feeling as though he were coming out of a trance. "She's heading for the western spring. I came to get you. The attackers are after Father and our family."

"We know." Branwen brushed his hair back and kissed his forehead. "They gathered us together. They're killing the men on sight. Whoever spread the fire woke the whole camp and gave people time to scatter, but we don't know if..." Her voice trailed away as tears filled her eyes.

Nocien shook her off as gently as he could and gave them what he hoped was his most serious gaze; in his mind, he could feel Father Cadfen behind him. "Mother Rhonwen, you're wounded. Go to the spring and find Tegwen; she's alone and unarmed. I'll follow as soon as I have Father and the other mothers."

Rhonwen stared at him, her eyes dark in the flickering shadows. Eurwen was the one who agreed, making the motion of acceptance with her hands; they *did* need to leave, and Nocien could follow after finding Cadfen and the others. Rhonwen sighed and nodded, pausing only as she passed to press her hand to his shoulder, her whisper catching at the base of her throat. "Come find me, my own flesh and blood."

Eira pressed a quick kiss to his cheek, shifting her grip on Mabyn as she carried her out. "Be safe." Nocien nodded and tried not to look her or Tesni in the eye. He didn't want to cry. When they melted into the night, it was easier. He might die, but that was a fear he could handle, a smaller thing than watching a stranger with a strange sword menace his mothers and sisters. Now he just had to find his father.

He followed the sounds of fighting, creeping into the center of camp. Crawling to stay out of sight, he poked his head out from under a collapsed tent and had to fight to keep his stomach from emptying itself. Bodies lay everywhere, and these were ones he knew all too well. He counted their names in his head without allowing himself to focus on where they'd fallen or the wounds they'd suffered: Ceinwen, the prettiest of the mothers; Meinwen, the bright gangly one who was all arms and elbows; Iolen, Emrys, Aneirin, and Morcant, his brothers. All four of his brothers, the sons of Cadfen, struck down and unbreathing.

Father fought in the center of the camp, a fierce whirling blade of fury. He was wounded and bleeding where a gash had been carved above his right knee, but he hadn't slowed yet. Men jabbed swords at him but his spear struck back and the bodies of their band littered the ground as testament to his skill.

For a heartbeat, Nocien allowed himself to hope. So many were dead and could never be replaced, but Father would kill the attackers and they would go in triumph to the survivors at the spring. They would know peace again and would rebuild. Then a fist reached down to grab him by the hair and haul him up. He yelped and sputtered at the unexpected assault, his cooking knife dropping uselessly from his hands.

"Guyon! Look what we have peeking out from under the tents. Another family member?"

Father's face fell as a man turned his gaze on Nocien. The stranger wore leather armor studded with metal that flashed in the light. His eyes were hard and the set of his lips cruel. "I see a resemblance," he said, studying

Nocien with interest. "One of yours, Cadfen? Stand down, for the sake of the child."

"No! Father, watch out!"

He shouted the warning as movement rose from behind Father. One of the men had circled quietly around when Cadfen stopped moving and now his blade stabbed forward. Father's face contorted with pain, one hand rising to touch the blood staining his chest before he fell to his knees and sagged to the ground. "*Father!*"

Nocien wasn't sure if he was crying or if the world was swimming. The armored man approached him without haste, his gloved hand gripping Nocien by the chin to turn his head. Studying his face, he noted the birthmark, the broad splash of color on Nocien's cheek, warm and red as wine. "So he *was* your father? Tell me, do you have any more brothers than these?" He jerked his head at the bodies. "Sons of Autarch Cadfen, I mean. I don't care about the rest of your kin brats."

This question made no sense until the man repeated it, his kinsman gripping Nocien's hair tighter and pulling his head back with a sharp painful tug. "No! My brothers... my brothers!" A sob escaped his throat, not knowing how to begin to mourn. "You killed my brothers."

The man they called Guyon studied him a moment longer, then released his chin and turned away. "Keep tracking the women," he ordered, pointing directions to the men clustered around him. "One of them may be pregnant with another son. Anything that so much as *looks* fertile, you kill it."

"What about this one?" The man holding Nocien shook him hard enough to rattle his teeth.

Guyon's lip curled with distaste as several of the remaining men made leering noises. "Fine. Do it quickly and get back to tracking the survivors."

Four of them dragged Nocien away from the firelight into the shadows and brush surrounding the camp. His arm was pinned hard against his back, fresh tears leaping to his eyes when he felt the bone fracture from their manhandling. But they'd pinned his right arm, not his left, and they'd taken him for a helpless thing and not a hunter in his own right. The dominant left hand he'd inherited from his mother darted out to grab a knife from a man's belt and stab it into the thick flesh of his thigh. A howl, a scrabble to hold blood inside a body no longer able to contain it, and Nocien was free and running into the night.

He didn't dare run to the spring, fearful of leading them to the others, so he ran south, pelting through brush that tore at him as sharply as any knife. Only once did he run into one of the attackers, beating his way through the fields looking for survivors. Nocien killed for the third time that night, but not before taking wounds of his own. He ran on, stumbling and falling when the soft light of false dawn filled the sky above.

When he woke some time later, the same ethereal light illuminated the gentle face that peered down at him. "This child is injured. Lykos, ride to fetch Phile and tell her to bring bandages."

Master Hilon's kinship abandoned their campsite at sunrise the morning after their scouts noticed the approach of Guyon and his kin. Nocien stayed behind, waiting high in a tree overlooking a pond on the outskirts of the cleared camp ground. Hidden among thick leaves, he rested and dozed in the summer heat, sipping at his water-skin and watching the dust on the horizon as it marched closer. They were coming.

Guyon and his kin marched into the camp just after noon. Men kicked at the smoldering fires, and Nocien listened with grim pleasure to their grumbling over all that had been burned rather than left behind for the invaders to use. Nocien had begged Master Hilon to pollute the wells in addition to destroying the food and goods they could not carry, but Hilon had drawn a line at poisoning earth to which his kin might one day return.

Watching from his perch, Nocien was troubled to realize that the kinship carrying blood-red banners was not entirely composed of fighting men. On the night they'd attacked Cadfen and his kin, Guyon had brought only men with him, but of course those men were not his entire kin. Nocien watched women scurry through the camp helping to pitch the tents, draw water, and start cooking fires. Their heads stayed down and their eyes trailed the ground; more than once Nocien saw a man raise his hand in anger to one of the women.

He bit back his fury and studied the bodies moving about the camp. Women of all ages lit fires and helped to pitch tents, from elderly grandmothers to tiny babies barely big enough to toddle. Nocien recognized none of them, not a sister or a mother among them, and wasn't sure how to feel. He didn't want his sisters and mothers to be captives of these men, but his heart ached at the loss of them. Master Hilon had sent scouts to look for them after Nocien had trusted him with his story, but by then the trail was cold.

His family was dead or lost on the wind. Even if by some miracle they were alive, the best he could do to help them was what he'd already planned: kill the warlord who so inexplicably sought their deaths. Nocien did not expect to survive the encounter, but should he escape after his kill he would look for them after tonight. For now, all he could do was wait while the sun dipped low in the sky and sank into the horizon's embrace.

The largest tent in the clearing was pitched near the center and marked with the biggest of the blood-red banners. Lit on all sides by campfires, it would be difficult to approach unseen. Nocien would wait until the fires burned low and the watchmen were sleepy. He could be patient and await the perfect opportunity to sneak in and kill Guyon where he lay. If the warlord died loudly, Nocien would have to fight his way out; if not, there was the slenderest of chances that he could slip away without anyone noticing.

A soft gasp brought him back to the moment, jerking his gaze down to the ground below his tree. Beneath him stood a girl, her arms holding a basket almost as big as herself, filled to the brim with clothes for washing. She stared up at him in the dim starlight with wide eyes and his heart sank.

Knowing he hadn't a moment to lose before she screamed, he dropped from the tree and touched a finger to his lips. "Shh!" he warned and then almost gasped aloud; the girl before him was his sister Eira.

"Please don't hurt me." Her whispered pleading was all wrong; she didn't recognize him, and he realized with a bittersweet pang that he was mistaken. She was the same height and build as Eira, but her hair was a glossier black and her eyes the color of stormy skies.

Nocien sighed and shook his head, trying not to let the disappointment he felt show on his face. "I'm not here to hurt you; my quarrel is with your autarch. You're their captive, aren't you?" The bruise blossoming around her right eye suggested as much, enough for him to hazard a hopeful guess.

She chewed on her lower lip and shot a fearful look behind her at the camp. "Yes."

He couldn't let her return to the camp after seeing him; she might warn them and everything would be ruined. "You can run away. Tonight. Right now. They won't come after you; they'll be busy with me."

Temptation flared in her eyes but she shook her head, lips set in a surprisingly stubborn line. "You think it's that easy? I don't know this land! I'd run out of water; I'd die."

"Take this!" He stepped closer; she dropped the basket in fear and he pressed his water-skin into her hands. "Head northeast and find the lightning-struck tree; there's a pool at its base with clean water. Then go east to the sea. You'll be safe and free."

He saw the hesitation in her face but her fingers closed possessively around the neck of the water-skin. "The penalty for trying to escape—"

"Guyon dies tonight." Despite his anxiety, he forced his voice to stay low. "They won't come after you. They'll be too busy dealing with me, or I'll be dead and they'll be fighting for leadership."

She snorted and looked away from him, her eyes dull and weary.

"Many people try to kill him, but none of them succeed. Why should you be any different?"

"I'm not one of his drunken kinsman looking for a brawl or a sleepy fighter caught by surprise in the night. I've trained for this. He killed my father, Autarch Cadfen, my brothers and my mothers." His heart beat faster with each heated word and Nocien knew he sought to convince more than just this girl. "Either he'll die at my hands or I'll die trying to kill him. I've sworn it on my name."

She stared at him, her eyes wide and unblinking. "What is your name?"

He softened at the question. "Nocien, son of Cadfen. What's yours?"

She risked another glance behind her, but they were alone. "They call me Flur. But my name is Ishild."

Nocien nodded his understanding, pronouncing her true name with care. "Ishild, please run. I can't let you go back to the camp and tell them I'm here. Go to the pool under the charred tree and then east to the sea."

Ishild hesitated a moment longer then nodded. "Good luck, Nocien, son of Cadfen," she whispered, then plunged into the brush without another word, running away from both him and the camp.

He had earned a reprieve but not a long one. The girl had been sent to wash clothes for the camp, away from the drinking wells. She would be expected to take some time, but they would want her back before the fires burned low. If they suspected her of running away they would rouse the camp to look for her, which meant torches and alert men carrying weapons, and the element of surprise lost entirely.

Yet if waiting were not an option, neither was simply storming in. With so many men still awake and moving about, he'd be spotted the moment he stepped into the clearing and cut down before he found Guyon. He needed a distraction, something to get the fighters away from the warlord's tent or to flush the warlord out of his tent to a place more easily accessible to Nocien's blade.

His eye fell on one of the fires dotting the perimeter of the camp, the flames casting shadows on the canvas of the nearby tents. Fire, he thought, the kernel of an idea taking root. Fire could be *very* distracting.

Canvas caught fire like dry kindling on the hot summer night, belching smoke and flame into the sky. Hidden in the brush, Nocien watched men scramble to contain the blaze, calling for buckets and water from the wells. Women were pushed aside and made to stand back; not, he decided, because the men wanted to protect them, but because they didn't trust the women not to spread the fire further.

The man who haunted Nocien's nightmares stormed from his tent as the flames roared louder. Guyon was in a state of undress, pulling his tunic over his graying hair as he stalked out. His sword-belt was fastened tight around his waist, Nocien noted, but his boots were laced only halfway up. He took in the chaos before him with a cold glance and spat out orders to the men who scurried about.

He wasn't alone and asleep as Nocien would have preferred, but distracted and unattended would have to do. Crouching low, he stepped swiftly through the brush and into the perimeter of the camp. Campfires bathed him in light, but the kinsmen were too busy in their rushing panic to notice one quiet stranger. He gripped his saber behind his back to avoid the gleam of metal catching his target's eye.

"Pull down the bordering tents so they can't catch! No, pull them *away* from the fire! You!" The warlord turned as he gestured towards flapping canvas, his eyes falling on Nocien. "Get a bucket and help, boy!"

Nocien wondered if he might be able to play the part as a ruse to get closer, but the man's eyes were already narrowing with suspicion. Nocien looked out of place here because he *was*; he was a stranger with his hands behind his back and a flagrant disregard for the fire threatening to set the camp ablaze. Perhaps, too, the hate in his eyes could only be tamped down so far before it boiled over.

"You're not one of my men." Guyon pulled his blade from his belt in an instant but he did not leap forward to attack. He watched Nocien with wary interest, as if trying to place him. "Where do I know you from?"

The advantage of surprise lost, Nocien brought his blade from behind his back. Another step closed the distance between them, his eyes darting between Guyon's blade and his surroundings. "You see in my face the family you butchered," he spat, his hands trembling as he held his blade. So long anticipating this moment and now he was here. He needed to be absolutely perfect.

The warlord had the audacity to chuckle. "I've butchered my fair share. Help an old man with his aging memory."

"Two years ago." He took another step, circling around to watch for anyone sneaking up on him. Guyon turned in his place easily, neither falling back or pressing ahead, just watching and waiting. "You killed my father, Autarch Cadfen, and my brothers, Iolen, Emrys, Aneirin, and Morcant. You killed his wives, my mothers. We had done *nothing* to you, and you slaughtered them in the night. Now you pay."

For the span of a heartbeat, Guyon's eyes widened and Nocien saw fear in those depths. Then recognition dawned and terror was replaced by disdain. "I know you. That wine-red birthmark splashed over your cheek; you're the girl who got away. You came back to torch my camp?" He shook his head and slashed the air with his sword, warming his muscles. "Child, you've made the worst decision of your short life."

The man leaped forward but tension in his foot gave away the attack and Nocien met him with steel. Saber and sword clashed with a jangling note that rang through the camp, the sound of battle unmistakable even in competition with the roaring flames. Nocien knew he had to finish this quickly and lashed in a wild strike, leaving himself unforgivably open to the shame of Master Hilon were he there to see. Guyon met the strike with an easy parrying blow and the fighters parted to circle one another again.

68

Nocien was lucky to be unbloodied after such an impetuous swing, but confusion outweighed his relief; his opponent ought to have taken advantage of his error. Guyon's circling movements struck him as odd. The man was clearly no beginner with a sword, yet his feints and jabs read as far in advance to Nocien as if they'd been called out in warning. This was nothing like a duel with Master Hilon and barely like one with Lykos; Guyon seemed bored, as though he were so confident of the outcome that he felt no inclination to waste his efforts.

Perhaps the closeness of his men made him arrogant. Yet even as they rallied around the fighters and Nocien's heart sank, the warlord waved them away. "She's only a girl," he announced to knowing chuckles.

Nocien's lip curled in a sneer that looked braver than he felt as his saber struck metal with another jarring clang. "You claim not to fear girls, Guyon? You weren't so courageous when you slaughtered my mothers, Ceinwen and Meinwen. They never did you any harm but you cut them down like the coward you are."

Guyon's blade met his easily as men jeered and laughed around them; as lackluster as he was with his half-hearted attacks, the man's parrying strikes were a testament to skill. Worse, Nocien's taunts hadn't riled him into making a careless opening. "Child, the only threat those women represented lay in their wombs."

"Why?" The cry ripped from Nocien's throat as he flung himself into another attack, less reckless than before but still parried with ease; he was tiring, he could feel it, and he hadn't so much as drawn blood against the older man. "What possible threat could a baby be, you monster?"

The warlord struck with more force, the impact shuddering up Nocien's arm as his saber met the attack. "Not a baby; a *son* of Autarch Cadfen. That is why *you*, girl, are not a threat, because *no* girl is a threat. The greatest soothsayer in the north swore I could only be killed by Cadfen's son, and that line is broken!"

Guyon's final word was a roar of triumph. His sword lashed out and

Nocien reeled away, jerking backwards as Master Hilon had taught him and narrowly escaping the blow. Not quite, he realized a moment later, as the sting set in and spectators cheered; the wound was shallow, but blood wept from a puncture to his stomach. He slapped his hand to the cut but his mind was occupied with the words still washing over him.

Helplessly, Nocien began to laugh.

The sound was shrill in his ears, almost manic with raw hilarity. Guyon watched with bored eyes, and somehow this made the situation even more funny. Shaking his head and choking back guffaws, Nocien brought his gaze to meet the man who had wounded him, who had murdered his family, and who would almost certainly be the death of him. Nocien was now perfectly confident he would return the favor.

"What's so funny, girl?" Guyon's voice was as bored as his gaze. "The thought of your impending doom?"

Nocien snorted, his hand tightening on the hilt of his blade. "You never realized." He laughed once more, a ragged burst of air he couldn't hold back. "Guyon, I *am* a son of Cadfen. His last son, the sole survivor. And you've given me every reason to kill you."

A heartbeat passed as Guyon's eyes widened and his misplaced confidence fled. His sword-arm faltered in a tiny, uncertain dip and Nocien saw his chance. Lunging forward on the balls of his feet, he let his body close the distance his shorter arms could not. His saber sliced through the man's tunic to the skin underneath and carved a wide path from armpit to armpit; as blood began to flow like summer rain, he flashed a brilliant smile at the shocked man. "I'll admit that *your* impending doom gave me a chuckle as well."

The body of the man whose existence had so marred Nocien's own crumpled to the ground before him, the last expression on his face one of pained astonishment. Nocien turned, clutching the wound in his stomach, and regarded the men surrounding him. They too seemed shocked by the death of their leader, but he knew that would not last. The men would rally, capture, and kill him, and he could only hope to take a few of them with him before he succumbed.

Or so Nocien thought until the first spear drove through the chest of one of the men, followed by the shouts of invaders rushing the camp from the surrounding darkness.

He thought they were ghosts, or the visions of a dying man succumbing to a wound that must have been more serious than he realized. Then battle joined and there was no time to think, only the flash and clash of metal. Men fell to the onslaught of spears he knew as intimately as his own hands, and those who tried to run found their throats cut with slender knives wielded by women they'd kept in captivity. Screams rent the air and the scent of blood and smoke and fire overwhelmed his senses.

Nocien found himself lying on his back on the ground, his head cradled in Mother Rhonwen's lap as Mother Tegwen tended to the wound in his stomach with her gentle hands. Eira handed her bandages while little Mabyn clung to Tesni, who had shot up almost as tall as Nocien in the time since he'd last seen her. Branwen and Eurwen moved about dousing fires and communicating with the camp women. Eurwen was having an easier time with her hands than Branwen was with her words, finding the captive women did not all speak the same language.

"How did you know where to find me?" Nocien's voice sounded ragged in his ears, his throat raw from smoke. "I didn't know where to look for you. Master Hilon sent scouts but so much time had passed—"

Rhonwen shushed him, leaning over to kiss his forehead. "We didn't. Forgive me, my own heart, but when you didn't return we were certain that you were dead. We've been on the move ever since, picking up kinsfolk who ran that night wherever we could find them. We stayed on the move to avoid the warlord, for we knew he was hunting us. He has been scouring the land while we struggled to hide from his scouts."

"He believed one of Father's sons would kill him," Nocien tried to explain. Soothsayers were rare and not a part of his life in either Cadfen's kinship or Hilon's, but Guyon must have had access to one. Did the soothsayer know that his prophecy would cause the death of so many in Nocien's family, or would all this have happened without his prediction? Nocien couldn't begin to guess.

"I know." Tears streamed over Rhonwen's cheeks as she bent again to kiss him. "My beautiful, brave boy. Ishild told us, and I couldn't run here quickly enough."

Nocien was light-headed from loss of blood, and the soft onslaught of his mother's kisses did little to halt the spinning of the stars above. "Ishild? The laundry girl?"

The girl poked her face out from behind Eira at the sound of her name, watching with wary eyes. "They caught me running from the camp. I told them about the prophecy Guyon always bragged about, how he could only be killed by Cadfen's son."

"And she told us about the boy who sent her running," Tegwen said, shaking her head with a soft smile as she worked. "A child of Cadfen carrying a wine-stain birthmark on his cheek. Who else could it be but you?"

"You came to rescue me," Nocien breathed, lost in the happy warmth of his mothers' hands. "You brought your spears to save me and the captive women."

Rhonwen wiped tears from her face and smiled, a fierce huntress once more, embodying everything he'd feared never to see again. "Yes. Some of us have wanted to attack for a while. We knew we couldn't run forever, so we thought to take the fight to him and win or die together, but we disagreed on the time and place. You forced our hand with flame and steel, and I could not be more proud of my strong son."

"He'll be stronger in the morning," Tegwen declared as she finished binding his wound. "And then we can decide where to go from here, or whether to stay a while. It's a nice campsite."

"East." Nocien's voice was a soft whisper. He smiled up at them, drifting away on a warm haze as the pain ebbed to a low throb. "Tomorrow we travel east, to the sea. There's kin there I want you to meet." His smile widened at the idea of seeing Master Hilon again. "You'll like them, I know."

Daughter of Kings

Content Note: Misgendering, Parental Bigotry, mention of Parental Death

"Finnnnnnnnnnnnnnnnnnnn! Where aaaaaaare you?"

Finndís twisted in her saddle at the bellow of her nickname. Giving a light clench on the rein and a nudge of her heel against the horse's barrel, she moved her gelding around to face the howl on the wind. Beside her, Torjei's spine unconsciously stiffened as he sat straighter and whirled his horse in time with her quick movements.

"Is that Rúni hollering?"

She nodded in response, her eyes narrowed against the afternoon sun as she searched the hills behind them. There; the telltale gallop of a horse and the sight of her little brother cresting the green horizon. He was alone—a thing the young prince ought never be—and riding his horse hard, leaning into the animal as he squeezed his legs into its sides for more speed. Finndís felt her breath catch in her throat and urged her ride forward at a brisk canter to meet the little prince and his frantic steed.

The boy's mare tossed her head and shied away from the approaching geldings. Finndís scowled; the dun mare was the most willful beast in the stables and she had begged Father not to give her to Rúni. She touched her heel to turn but before her gelding could correct course Torjei was there,

74

hands reaching to secure the mare's bridle and draw her to a reluctant halt. "Rúnolfur! What are you doing out of the castle?"

"Is there an emergency? Is Father ill?" Finndís drew to a stop along the other side of Rúni, framing the mare between their two geldings and sparing Torjei the briefest glance of gratitude. Torjei was faithful to a fault, the best shield-brother and companion she could ask for, and always wherever she needed him.

Rúni looked up at her with wide eyes, grinning without the slightest trace of repentance. "What? No, I'm *bored*. Can I come hunting with you? Pleeeeease? Look, I brought my bow and everything!"

Inarticulate exasperation rattled in Torjei's throat as he bit back oaths he could not utter. Some familiarity was expected between the young nobleman and the royal family in whose keeping he'd been raised as an official companion for the regal children, but swearing at the littlest prince over his antics would cross a subtle line.

"Is that a 'yes'?" Rúni pressed with a dazzling grin, tickled by Torjei's obvious anger.

Finndís stared at the boy, blinking as her heart slowed and she tried to form a coherent response. "No, you can't come hunting with us. Rúni, where is your tutor? You should be at your lessons!"

Her little brother twisted his lips into a sour face, fidgeting in the saddle while Torjei held the mare's rein tight. "Master Gunnulf told me to go play. He's visiting with Father and the clan-lords; they were emptying the wine cellar when I left, and Master was deep in his cups. So if you think about it, I wasn't running *away* from lessons, I was running *to* them. You can teach me more than that grizzled old boar, Finn!"

Torjei snorted in derision, glad to have a safe target at which to direct his lingering ire. "Worthless cur! He shouldn't be drinking with lords, let alone sending you off unsupervised so he could join the party. Why your father hired him is a mystery; the only lesson he can teach is how to reach the bottom of a bottle."

"Torjei." Finndís took the rein on her side of the mare with a gentle hand and motioned for Torjei to hand over the other. Rúni fidgeted again at this, not liking the silent implication that he was too much of a baby to hold his own reins, and the high-strung mare danced restlessly in place underneath him. "They fought in the war together. Father was a young man and Gunnulf was loyal to him and Grandmother. Most of our visiting lords were on her side, too; noble or not, he shares a bond with them which we ought to respect. He should not have let you leave the castle alone, however," she added, shooting a stern look at Rúni.

"Well, he didn't actually know I was leaving," Rúni hedged, not meeting her eyes. "He told me to play and I thought you two might like my help! Anyway, he's still an awful tutor, no matter how loyal he is."

"Father didn't hire him for his loyalty," corrected Finndís in a weary voice, shaking her head as she looped his reins around the front rings of her saddle and urged the horses in the direction of the castle. They were wasting precious daylight taking Rúni back, but she didn't trust him to go by himself. If they went at a steady canter, there would still be time to bring down a doe or a brace of rabbits for the lords to sup on.

Torjei matched their pace, riding alongside her with effortless skill. "Though if he had, no one could blame him," he added in an undertone, his dry humor restored. "The quality seems in short supply nowadays."

She ignored him, hoping Rúni would not catch his words and fire off a thousand questions in response; the intrigues of clan-lords were not something she wished to inflict on her little brother. "Gunnulf has witnessed history firsthand, Rúni. He knew our father as a youth and fought beside him in the war; he has seen a side of Father that you or I have never known. There is much you could learn from him, if you tried."

The boy turned sorrowful eyes up at her, though she suspected the root cause of his despair lay in being led back to the castle against his will instead of allowed out on the afternoon hunt. "But he's not a *real* tutor; not like the ones Father provided for you, Finn. I don't think he likes me at all!"

Torjei snorted again. He had a vast plethora of snorts at his disposal, and Finndís knew each one as intimately as the callouses on her hands; this one mingled amusement with grudging fondness. "Can you blame Master Gunnulf if he doesn't like you? Considering how often you run off, I'd think anyone—"

"Not Master Gunnulf! Father! *He* doesn't like me!"

Finndís whipped around to stare at the wailing child, her jaw dropping as a thousand false reassurances crowded into her mouth and faltered at the precipice. Father *didn't* like Rúni, but that was because he rarely thought of him at all. Rúni's existence did not offend the distant king; the boy simply didn't matter to him.

Silence was damning so Finndís spoke; in her gentlest tone, she tried to soften the truth. "Father doesn't dislike you, Rúni. He loves you. You should have seen how he held you as a baby." This was stretching the truth a bit more than she ought, but his wide eyes lapped up the lie as he leaned closer to catch her words. "If he neglects us sometimes, it's because he's so busy being king."

Beside her, Torjei nodded with a solemn expression. He was not as skilled as she with soothing words, but on the subject of absent fathers he could commiserate mightily. "That job would turn any man's hair gray, Rúni. He's got to run the kingdom while half the lords consider him a temporary regent at best and an illegitimate usurper at worst. And your elder brothers aren't making his life easier. If he didn't have all that on his plate, you can bet he'd be out here hunting with us and teaching you how to use that bow properly."

Finndís wiped doubts from her face as Torjei's rosy vision coaxed a fresh smile from the little prince. "You think so? Oh, Finn, tell me the story about Grandmother Ásdís and the uncles, and how Father became king! Maybe the three of us can get the lords to stop fighting, and then Father can go hunting with us! Please?"

This was a stalling tactic to slow the ride home, one often used at night to beg one last tale before bed. Finndís gave the boy a skeptical look and glanced up at Torjei in time to see him bite back a smile; her shield-brother was as fond of hearing her tell stories as Rúni was of demanding them. "You'd know our history as well as I do if you listened to Master Gunnulf and paid attention to your lessons."

"But you tell it better than he does," cajoled Rúni, teeth flashing in a flattering grin. "Go on, Finn, please tell the story. If you do, I'll be quiet the whole walk back, and I'll go inside the castle when we get there, and be good. I won't even sneak into the great hall to watch the clan-lords drink with Father, I promise."

"And pigs will sprout wings and fly," Finndís grumbled, giving him a sharp look. She took a deep breath and sat higher in her saddle, feeling like a bard attending a banquet at which she'd not intended to perform yet had been called upon without warning. "Very well, I'll tell the story; but I'm holding you to that oath, Rúni."

Finndís let her voice settle into a warm cadence that rose and fell in time with her horse's gait, the same lulling rhythm used by the traveling storytellers who plied their trade during winter in exchange for a seat by the hearth. "A long time ago, when dragons roamed the land—"

"Dragons still roam the land!"

She turned her head to glare at Rúni. "You said you'd be quiet. And, no, they don't."

Rúni was undeterred. "I can't stay quiet if the story is *wrong*, Finn! What about the last harvest-hunt?"

Torjei shook his head, chuckling; Finndís had long ago noticed he managed to find Rúni's antics much more amusing when they only inconvenienced her and not him. "That was a scrawny little scrap of a lizard, barely older than you, boy. We chased it north out of the fields. One or two sightings a year isn't the same."

"Well, they do still roam the land!"

Finndís shushed him with a hiss. "*Fine.* A long time ago, when *packs* of dragons still roamed the land, you could hardly keep sheep or pigs because they'd be eaten, and sometimes the shepherd too. Better?"

"Go on," Rúni said, the soul of solemn magnanimity, as Torjei turned red biting back a guffaw.

Finndís gave her shield-brother a sharp look, reflecting as she always did how lucky he was to be so handsome. Not being a child of royal blood, he had been allowed to participate in his fair share of friendly duels and his face already sported two beautiful scars across his left cheek, the deep craters proof of his bravery. She shook her head at both boys and averted her gaze before Torjei could catch her staring.

"The clans were divided," she continued, finding her vocal stride again. "Dragons and bears and wolves killed herds in the night. Bandits and brigands killed men. The people looked for a hero to lead them."

"Ooh, ooh!" Rúni leaned forward in his saddle, eyes sparkling with eager attention. "Grandmother Ásdís!"

She thinned her lips but didn't scold him for the interruption, deciding that if Rúni couldn't be coaxed into sitting still for his lessons, perhaps he could be tricked into them. "Yes, Grandmother Ásdís and her golden sword. Do you remember the names of her three sons?"

The trick fell flat, passing over his head like an arrow sailing beyond its target. "No. Where'd the sword come from? A great golden sword like that must have come from somewhere."

"It... came from the gods," hazarded Finndís, offering the official explanation with the slightest pause; Father was devout enough in his own way, but she'd yet to see anything in her own mundane life to convince her that such divine beings existed or cared about the affairs of the tiny humans below.

"Or from an extremely adept wand-wife," Torjei tossed in cheerfully, pushing his long dark hair from his face as the wind picked up behind them. "Or she found it in a dragon's hoard, or stole it from a sage."

Rúni stared at them, frowning as no further explanation came. Finndís swiped at strands of her own fiery hair as they whipped on the breeze and stuck to her lips. "No one knows for sure," she explained, hoping this would satisfy the boy. "Queen Ásdís only ever said it was magic and came to her."

This did not entirely placate her audience; Rúni sagged backwards in his saddle with great drama and sighed loudly. "Okay, okay. She slew dragons with her sword and the clans crowned her queen."

Finndís felt her lips twitch and held back a smile. "Well, it was a little more complicated than that. Master Gunnulf is supposed to be teaching you the names of the clan-lords and the dates they joined under her banner. But, yes, she united our people and made the land a safe place for us to thrive. She took a husband from among the clan-lords and bore him three sons. Do you remember their names?" she pressed.

Rúni fidgeted again. "Nooooo."

"There's a mnemonic," she urged, trying not to sound impatient. "S-O-N, for son. Now do you remember?"

He shook his head and Torjei caught her eye, lifting his chin and looking every inch the dashing son of a clan-lord. "I know!" he volunteered, all exuberant enthusiasm. "Finn, ask me. *I* know them by heart."

Rúni looked up sharply at Torjei's bragging, sitting straight in his saddle. "I never said I didn't know!" he lied, anxious not to be upstaged. "S is for, um, Uncle Sveinn."

Finndís nodded, smiling warmly. "And you know N already," she encouraged.

"King Njáll!" Their father's name burst from his lips in a proud boast. "And, uh, Uncle Orvur?"

"Orvar," she corrected, her wide grin praising both the boy's triumph and Torjei's clever ruse. "You *did* know them all. We'll make a scholar of you yet, Rúni."

He blushed at the compliment, but his joy was dampened as they crested a hill and the castle rose into sight. Rúni sighed, the despondent sound almost lost on the wild spring breeze. "I know Father is king because the uncles were killed in the war, but that was a long time ago. Why doesn't he have time for me now? Didn't he have time for you and Magni and Leifur long ago when you were little like me?"

Finndís hesitated, glancing at Torjei for help he could not provide. The problem was that Rúni was right; Father *did* have less time for the boy than he'd had for his older three children. Rúni ought to have more and better tutors than Master Gunnulf, and he should have an official companion as Finndís had Torjei. The reasons for his neglect lay in the events surrounding the end of the war, and in prophecies which had reverberated through the following years and shaped the politics of their kingdom. Yet these reasons wouldn't lessen Rúni's hurt when he learned them. Finndís took a softer tone, letting her horse slow.

"Grandmother Ásdís turned over control of the kingdom to her eldest son while she still lived, in an attempt to secure an orderly succession," she said, letting her cadence weave a measure of distance around their family's shame. "But Sveinn was a disastrous king, alienating the clans as soon as he was crowned. Orvar gathered western lords to attack him, starting a civil war and nearly destroying the kingdom in the process. Grandmother Ásdís did all she could to halt the war, but when the brothers would not stand down she rode out with Father and the eastern clans. They say her sword bathed the battlefield in golden light."

Rúni sat straighter in his saddle now, eyes wide as he listened.

"Sveinn and Orvar died in combat and bitter grief struck Queen Ásdís. While Father dealt with the clans, she rode into the heart of the Witchwoods and drove her sword into a stone. The lords found her that night at the edge of the woods, bearing grievous injuries on her body. She told them what she had done before she died. On that same night, every wand-wife and sage in the land prophesied a daughter of the queen's lineage would one day pull the sword from the stone and unite our clans under a single banner once more."

The boy tilted his head, frowning slightly. "But we have no daughters in our family, do we?"

Finndís couldn't answer and Torjei smoothed over the pause. "Since your grandmother died, your family has been in a race to produce one. King Njáll married before Ásdís was in the ground and turned out three sons as quickly as his bride could manage before she was taken by a winter chill." He glanced at Finndís, knowing the wound from losing her mother was still sharp. She was grateful for an excuse to turn her head.

He continued, carving space for her to gather herself as he distracted Rúni. "Your brothers Leifur and Magni wedded noblewomen as soon as they came of age, in the hopes that they would sire girls with their brides. Meanwhile, every lord standing in opposition to your father has spent the last three decades searching for a bastard daughter Sveinn or Orvar might have left behind, hoping to break the line of Njáll."

Rúni bit his lower lip, realization settling in at last. "And my mother? Father was trying to make a daughter with her? Not a boy like me?"

"She was a good woman, Rúni," Torjei said, his voice gentle. "Your father picked her from a dozen girls put forward by the clan-lords. She had kind eyes, green like yours, and she was patient with me and Finn. We liked her."

The boy nodded in a distracted way. His small body swayed lightly in the saddle with the movement of his mare and Finndís noticed with a pang that their easy canter had slowed to a walking pace. Precious time threatened to slip away but she was loath now to rush her little brother. "So that's why Father has no time for me? He's finding a new wife to be our mother so he can make a girl?"

Torjei thinned his lips. "Well, that's *one* of the problems on his plate. Every graybeard in the kingdom wants to be grandsire to the next queen, so they're pushing their daughters forward to compete for your father's hand, or for Leifur's now that he's a widower. Meanwhile, younger sons like you and me are bereft of attention from both our fathers and the ladies alike. You think you have it bad, boy, but Lady Inge was almost engaged to Finn here before her father broke it off in order to shove her at your father. Poor woman."

Finndís turned away again before Rúni could notice her blush. Truth be told, she had only spoken with Lady Inge on a handful of occasions, but the lady had been lovely in every possible way. Her warm eyes seemed to pierce the soul, and her smile always held a gentle little laugh in the corner of her lips. Finndís had been stunned when Inge's father halted the engagement proceedings, and her feelings on the matter were still a tangled skein of sorrow and hurt as she waited and hoped Njáll would not marry her.

"Is that why the clan-lords have come today?" asked Rúni, slipping into the thoughtless exuberance of youth and insensible to his sister's pain. "Are we going to have a wedding soon?"

She drew a deep breath and shoved thoughts of Lady Inge aside, licking her lips as she considered how to answer; here was departure from history into the intrigues from which she'd hoped to protect her brother. "Father is struggling to maintain control," she explained, picking each word with care. "Some lords regard Leifur as heir because he is firstborn, and wish to rally around him. Others look to Magni, as his wife birthed a daughter over Candletide. Sigdís is only a few months old but Magni is demanding to be made regent, claiming that Father is unlikely to sire more children. The lords are meeting to discuss the future of the kingdom."

Torjei snorted, the soft sound suffused with disdain. "Magni is over-confident as ever, naming her heir-apparent when she won't be old enough to hold a sword for another decade or more. Anything could happen in that time, and there's no guarantee she's the daughter the sages swear is coming."

Rúni frowned at his words, biting at his lower lip in thought. "So Sigdís won't be accepted as queen until she grows up and pulls Grandmother Ásdís' sword from a stone sitting in the middle of the Witchwoods?"

"That's the long and short of it, boy," Torjei agreed, but his attention was on Finndís. He rode beside her, watching her in the gentle way he always had. She lifted her head to meet his gaze, wondering if the gratitude she felt for him showed through the pain he saw in her face.

Her brother interrupted before her mouth could open. "That's not far from here. I want to see!"

His hands tugged on the reins she'd tied off onto her saddle rings before his words penetrated her ears. The high-strung dun mare danced under the squirming boy as he lurched forward on her back. Runi's thrashing heels poked her sides and the mare squealed her displeasure, kicking out at Finndís' gelding. "Rúni, stop! You'll fright—"

With a final sharp tug he freed the mare's reins and settled hard back into his saddle. The mare kicked again and bolted, galloping over the hills towards the castle while the boy on her back fought to turn her towards the woods. Finndís had only a glimpse of this, for her gelding danced with restless distress after being kicked at and Torjei's horse gave an anxious whinny and backed away from the commotion.

Her heart in her mouth, she poured her concentration into staying seated and calming her mount. When both she and her gelding could breathe again, Rúni was gone. Digging her heels in, she urged her horse into the chase, saving her breath rather than gasp an order to Torjei. He would follow her, she knew.

The Witchwoods lay west of the castle, a dark gash in the countryside where trees grew so close together that sunlight never reached the ground. Pink heather sprawled across rolling fields between the woods and the castle, nourished by blood spilled there during the war of succession that ended with Njáll crowned king. Only the unwise entered the woods, for bears and wolves lurked there—and the superstitious said worse.

Finndís had never set foot in there, though she had gazed on those woods from her window all her life. Now she paced the edge of the forest on her gelding, her fists too tight on the reins as her heart pounded in her chest and her horse tossed his head in protest at the bit jabbing in his mouth. Sucking in a long calming breath, she forced her hands to relax on the reins and made herself wait.

Torjei straightened from where he bent to examine the earth then pulled himself back into his saddle. "Tracks go directly in," he reported, his lips thin.

Torn leaves and gouged earth marked the area where Rúni had plunged his mare into the woods, but Finndís had hoped against hope the boy might have followed the treeline around to the north rather than enter the dark forest. She sighed and cast a longing glance over her shoulder at the castle. "We can't leave him in there. I'll go after him while you head back to rouse the guards."

Torjei didn't look at her but sat straighter in the saddle. "I'm not leaving you. We can go for the guards or we can go in after him together." He flashed a grin at her then, dazzling and insouciant as ever. "Besides, you know I'm the better tracker."

Finndís glared at him, knowing he was right. "You realize you're supposed to actually carry out my orders sometimes, Torjei? Royal companions usually do."

His brilliant smile didn't falter for an instant. "If I left your side, I wouldn't be here to obey your every order. So where shall I follow you now: forest or castle?"

She ran a weary hand over her face, pushing back her hair and wishing she had something to tie it up with; the dark branches ahead looked likely to snare. "Faint heart never won," she murmured, allowing herself one last look back before gulping a deep breath and guiding her horse into the trees.

Sunlight vanished and she found herself in darkness as her eyes struggled to adjust. Her horse snorted, each step was tentative and she felt the breeze stir her hair and rustle the leaves above. Over the sound of the leaves she could hear a smattering of birdsong, but otherwise the forest was strangely quiet.

Her voice dropped to a hushed whisper. "Which way?"

"See the tracks there? He found an old hunting trail, or his mare did." Torjei pointed to indentations in the soft soil leading further into the woods. The tracks were wide apart and badly smeared, marking the mare's crashing progress, but at least the way was clear enough to indicate that Rúni had not been swept from his saddle.

Finndís sighed with relief, grateful to be spared a hunt for her brother's broken body. She guided her horse onto the trail with light touches, sensing the animal's nervousness. Torjei fell in line behind her, forced into single file by the tightly packed trees crowding both sides of the trail. His whisper drifted up to her on the breeze. "Finn, I'm sorry."

She wanted to turn her head to look back at him but didn't dare take her eyes from the trees ahead, not wishing to be knocked from her seat. "For what? Telling him Father wanted a daughter? He was going to put two and two together someday." She sighed and ducked under a low branch. "He took it well enough."

"No, I'm sorry I wasn't watching him." His voice, so low and serious, squeezed her heart.

"It's not your fault." She turned her head just enough for him to see her face in profile, hoping he could see she was not angry. "Torjei, he's my brother. I should have held his reins, but I didn't want to treat him like a baby. I ought to have been watching him and not allowed myself to be distracted."

"You're being unfair to yourself. That topic is painful for you, I know."

Finndís swallowed the sudden lump in her throat, unable to speak for fear her voice would crack. Torjei let the silence stretch between them for a long moment before going on. "I *do* know, Finn. We grew up together. I know you better than anyone else; better than your father or brothers, or the cooks or nursemaids. I know your heart, and I've never forgotten what you told me when I was brought here."

She must not cry. Whatever else happened, she would *not* cry in the Witchwoods while seeking her lost brother. But her eyes swam, remembering that first night when Torjei had sobbed himself to sleep in their shared room. She'd comforted him as best she could and they'd whispered secrets in the dark, promising always to stand by one another as friends even when the capricious adults around them did not.

"Father never believed me," she whispered, so softly she wasn't sure he heard. "I told him when I was younger than Rúni, still just a baby. He thought I'd heard Leifur and Magni talking about the prophecy, but I hadn't known anything about it. I wouldn't have cared even if I had! I didn't want to be a queen or hold a magic sword, I just wanted him to stop calling me something I wasn't. I wanted him to *see* me."

His voice was gentle behind her. "I see you, Finn. Your father is a king, not a god or a seer or even particularly wise; he's wrong as often as any other man. We'll find Rúni, take him home, ride out this council meeting with smiles painted on, and everything will be back to normal in a month."

She took a shaky breath and tried on a smile that almost fitted her face. "Agreed, but I'm going to lock Rúni in his rooms when we get back to the castle. How could he possibly have thought this was a good idea after hearing how Grandmother Ásdís was mortally wounded in these woods? Little fool!"

Torjei's chuckle was as dry as ever. "He's a lonely little boy, Finn. He needs a companion. Maybe one of the visiting lords has a brat his age whom he can be persuaded to leave behind. Don't worry too much; he has his bow and knows how to use it, and it's early spring which means that the bears are still asleep."

"I'm worried for a reason!" Anxiety made her voice sharp; they were setting a slower pace than Rúni and wouldn't catch up with him at this rate unless he stopped to wait. She didn't dare go faster, not wishing to risk one of the horses breaking a leg or herself being struck by a low-hanging branch. "There are wolves in here, even if the bears are still hibernating.

And *something* killed Queen Ásdís. Even without her magical sword, she wouldn't have been easy prey; some dragon or druid attacked her."

Her companion's voice took on a soft lull, calm as much for her sake as for the skittish horses. "Or she was wounded in the battle that took two of her sons, and no one noticed while she stole away to discard her weapon. Finn, he's going to be fine. Magic and monsters are the stuff of bedtime stories, and there are certainly none so close to your father's castle—"

A yell rent the silence of the forest, a high-pitched shriek of pain. Finndís gasped and heeled her horse into as much of a run as she dared, throwing caution to the wind at the mental image of her little brother broken and bleeding in her arms. "Rúni, hang on! We're coming for you! Where are you?"

"Finn, wait!"

She heard Torjei's shout behind her but was too far gone to care. Flattening herself along her horse's neck, she urged the creature faster, following the path of broken branches and muddied tracks Rúni had left in his wake. After what seemed an eternity, the trees widened out before her into a small clearing. The dun mare, bereft of rider and wearing an empty saddle, whinnied at the sight of her, happy to become the best of friends now that she was lost in the woods with no stable in sight.

"Where's Rúni?" Finndís knew it was nonsense to question an animal, but fear made her frantic. Her eyes darted around the clearing; no wolf surged from the shadows to attack her, no blood marked the ground where a body might have been dragged away. But there on the ground was a heavy indentation deep enough to mark where a small boy might have fallen from a saddle. "You *threw* him?"

Torjei thundered into the clearing behind her, wheeling his horse to a halt and petting its shoulder as it snorted at the sudden stop. Finndís whirled on him, her breath coming in short gasps. "She threw him. Look! She threw him, and I don't know why or where he is."

He was on his feet in an instant, kneeling at the edge of the soft earth. "Probably a snake," he suggested, glancing at the skittish dun mare, "or something in the undergrowth that startled her. He walked away afterwards, so he can't have been too badly hurt. He must've been dazed or seen something he wanted a closer look at."

"What could he possibly..." Her voice trailed off as she studied the edges of the clearing. On the western side, a speckled stone glinted on the ground; flat against the mossy grass, the stone was the breadth of her boot. Another lay beyond it and another past that, like a glittering garden path set by fairies. Finndís blinked at the stones. "What is that?" she whispered.

Torjei turned to stare at the path, his eyes widening in matching surprise. "Whatever it is," he observed with a deep frown, casting a worried glance back at her, "Rúni's tracks lead straight towards it."

Glittering cobblestones caught what little light filtered through the canopy and led them along a winding path through thick brush. They crept along on foot, having left the horses behind in the clearing with their reins looped around branches and their bits dropped so they could graze; the beasts were too large to thread their way along the gleaming path. As they approached an enormous tree bathed in shadow, Finndís was startled to hear Rúni's happy chirrup, high and easy, coming from *within* the tree.

His words were muffled and indistinct but he sounded perfectly content, and seemed to be speaking to someone. Finndís shot Torjei a worried glance as she stepped silently forward, her hand resting on the heavy hilt of her knife. In the shadows she could discern the faintest outline of a door: a flap of tanned skin lying flat against the bark of the trunk, almost the same color and texture. She reached out, letting her fingers graze the weather-beaten skin, then slipped inside.

At first she thought she'd stepped into a blaze. A fire burned in the center of the hollow tree, flames licking happily at a hanging cauldron, while the walls of the trunk glowed with a reddish light resembling embers in a dying hearth. Yet though the room was warm, she felt no pain and inhaled no smoke; soft breezes carried the steam from the bubbling cauldron through holes bored in the bark above her head. When she looked closer, blinking as her eyes adjusted, Finndís was surprised to realize the flickering glow coating the walls was a strange moss studded with the heads of tiny luminescent mushrooms.

"—so I asked Father to give her to me for my tooth-gift, and he did! She's the prettiest mare in the stable and the fastest horse we own, even if she *is* a little wild. I should be getting back to her, though."

"Let her graze a while longer; I told her to stay, and the clearing is safe by day. There is a pixie ring in the far corner and they dance round the toadstools at night, but twilight is far off and your mare is perfectly content for the time being. Now we must tend to another guest."

"Finn!"

Rúni sat on the floor at a low table that dominated the right side of the room and which was big enough for a man to stretch out upon and sleep; indeed, perhaps that was its use, for Finndís saw no bed and glimpsed rolls of thick fur bundled under the table as though stored away for the daytime hours. Rúni gripped a wide cup in both hands, the watery contents of which still smeared his chin, and beamed a bright smile at Finndís.

She tensed, expecting him to bowl into her with a hug, and was surprised when he did not. Her eyes fell on the wrappings tied about his left ankle. "Rúni! Are you hurt?" She wanted to run to him but refrained as she watched the owner of the unfamiliar voice, a strange shape hunched opposite him at the table.

She was a witch, for there could be no other word for her. Her ash-blond hair was straggly and hung in dirty clumps dotted with leaves and twigs. Her face was young but unnaturally pale and marred with pockmarks which spoke of hard living; a deep scar in her lip gave her smile a sinister twist. When she spoke, however, her words were solicitous. "He's fine; just a twisted ankle. Painful, but soon mended. I welcome you and your man to my home."

Finndís twisted to see Torjei lifting the skin covering the door behind her, then whipped back as the witch unfolded herself from the floor. A wooden wand the length of her forearm hung from her belt and swayed lightly as she pulled herself to her feet. Finndís forced herself not to take a step back, but watched the woman's hands in case they strayed towards the magical tool.

Politeness seemed prudent; Finndís gave a deep bow, keeping her eyes on the woman. "I thank you for tending to my brother," she said in a formal tone, anxious to express gratitude without incurring debt.

"Oh, it were no trouble," observed the witch with a smile. "Not the first little lost bird I've tended. If their wings don't mend they make a good stew, but this one will be fine; just a bad fall."

"We nearly trampled her!" Rúni put in cheerfully. "Rode into the clearing and *whoa* she was there, and my mare shied and threw me! The whole time she didn't flinch at all, Finn, just watched us. You never saw anyone so brave!"

Finndís blinked at his account and nodded in a cautious manner. "I am very grateful you are both safe. Now we need to get you home; Father will be worried. Come, we'll carry you back to the horses."

"But I haven't finished my broth!" The boy kicked up an instant fuss as Finndís had known he would, but Torjei moved around her and gathered him up in his arms in spite of the stream of complaints. Torjei knew as well as she that they must get Rúni away from the witch before she brought any harm to him.

Finndís watched the woman as Torjei struggled with the writhing boy, but she seemed wholly uninterested in the scuffle at her table. Her attention remained focused on Finndís and the two women stared at each other with matching intensity. While Finndís' gaze was wary, the witch seemed almost amused.

"I see you in my dreams." The words were offered without preamble.

"Excuse me?"

Her smile grew wider and the red glow of the strange flickering moss reflected off two rows of surprisingly numerous teeth. Finndís tried to picture her in full sunlight, wondering if she only appeared sinister through a trick of the shadows, but her imagination failed her; the woman did not fit into a world of bright meadows and warm castle halls. "I see you in my dreams. I can't think I'm the only one. May I know your name? I already know your brother's, but you are far more interesting to me."

Torjei looked up sharply but Finndís needed no warning; only the unwise gave their name to a witch. Rúni, determined to prove this adage, ceased his struggle in Torjei's arms and grasped the opportunity to be helpful. "That's Finn! Torjei, let me down; I don't want to go! Finn, tell him to put me down!"

Finndís swallowed hard against the lump in her throat, but the damage was done. She nodded at the witch, easing her feet back a step towards the doorway, anxious to leave. "I am called Finn, madam." The familiar diminutive was incomplete but not incorrect, and more than the woman needed to know.

The woman shook her head and the amusement in her eyes gleamed brighter. "You may be called Finn, but that is not your name. To know your name is surely a small thing to ask after binding this little one's ankle."

"We must go—" Torjei started, his voice a commanding boom in the small space, but Rúni squirmed in his arms again, confused and anxious to clear away any misunderstandings with his benefactress.

"Do you mean our long names? Mine's Rúnolfur, but everyone calls me Rúni. Finn's long name is Fin—"

"No." The witch's eyes all but danced now as she watched Finndís. "I wish to know your *true* name."

Finndís stared at her as the world slowed. Shadows drew closer around them until they were the only two living creatures in the world. Torjei

92

was gone, swallowed by the darkness; Rúni's chirruping voice no longer reached her ears. There was only herself and the witch, and a long wand of thin white wood that dangled at her side and glowed with inner light against the encroaching void.

"My name is Finndís."

Her words were a whisper, the secret slipping over her lips like water over northern cliffs. She'd held the word close to her heart, sharing it with no one all these years. Not even Torjei knew, though she believed he'd suspected the truth when she first asked him to call her Finn and never the formal name Father used. But her own name, her *true* name, had been hers alone until this moment.

The witch smiled and the amusement in her eyes softened to something deeper and kinder. "An honor to meet you, Finndís, and to put a name to your lovely face. I am Eirný. Wand-wife Eirný, if you are feeling genteel; witch Eirný, if you are not. We are in the Witchwoods, after all, and I am at peace with my nature."

Light streamed into their world; only the glow of the moss and mushrooms and fire, but blinding after the darkness which had enveloped them. Torjei and Rúni stood nearby once more, staring at the two women, motionless save for their soft breathing; she did not know if they had overheard or if the words had been spoken in her mind alone. Eirný gave the trio a cheery smile, brushing loose dirt from her filthy robe.

"Well! Shall I show you the sword, then? I do think it's time."

There were a thousand reasons not to go deeper into the woods with a witch, and Finndís was troubled to find she had rationalized them all away. The trip would calm Rúni, who had flown into a fit when Torjei had at first refused to go. Flailing and kicking, the boy had sworn to sneak out of the castle and return in the night if they did not take him to see his grandmother's legendary sword. Torjei was strong enough to wrestle him back to the horses, of course, but his expression was grim and Finndís could guess why; they would have to inform King Njáll of Rúni's intentions, which would mean confessing this day's events to the stern lord.

Finndís had to admit, too, that she shared Rúni's curiosity. For all that the adults in her life spoke of the magic sword as something they'd seen in combat during their younger glory days, she had never quite shaken its air of myth from her mind. She thought of Grandmother's sword the way she thought of trolls and fairies: fantastical sights reserved for the eyes of those touched by magic and wonder. They were not for her, for the same reason the good silver dining set went unused when guests were not present.

So she had agreed to follow the witch deeper into the woods. Rúni had squirmed out of Torjei's arms and clasped her hand, following her like the gentle little lamb he wasn't. Torjei argued, but not for long and not convincingly; Finndís knew he shared their curiosity. He fell into line behind them as they squeezed through tight paths and followed the witch into darkness so deep it seemed like winter twilight in the forest rather than the spring noon they'd so recently left behind. All the while their guide chattered on like a bird, not seeming to notice or mind the silence pressing in on them from all sides.

"Don't come this way very often, at least not this time of year. Come back in autumn, though, and you'll see a riot of mushrooms near the stone. A few grow year-round, of course, but they're most plentiful after the autumn rains. No, round this time of year I keep to the outer woods. More meat; the animals don't forage this far in."

"Are there many witches in these woods?" Torjei's tone was strained and the question was pointed; he swiveled his head about as they walked, anxious of an ambush.

"Many witches in the Witchwoods?" Eirný sounded amused but evasive, letting the question roll over her tongue. "Well, yes and no. I suppose it depends who is counting and how they measure."

94

Finndís kept her tone gentle, feeling Torjei's irritation simmer behind her. "You have friends here, or relatives?" Her hand gripped Rúni's as they stepped over roots which threatened to trip them. The boy had been unusually silent since they'd left the house. Perhaps he was determined to behave himself as long as he got his way, but Finndís couldn't shake the worry that he knew her secret. Would he keep it, as Torjei had all these years, or would her name be the first thing on his lips when they returned home to Father?

A long pause ensued as the woman considered her words. "Your questions are not easy ones," she mused, almost to herself. "Hmm. You would not see another like me in these woods; there is your answer."

"Not a good one," muttered Torjei, as to Finndís' great relief the path ahead of them widened and opened into another clearing. She lifted Rúni over a high tangle of roots, the boy grunting like a happy pig as he scrambled with her, and then they were in a field of soft emerald grass dotted with little brown mushrooms. They grew in clusters around a gray stone dominating the very center of the clearing.

There could be no doubt that this was Queen Ásdís' stone. Twice Finndís' height, the four of them could join hands around it and still not complete the circle. A hilt jutted from the uneven rocky surface at a point just level with her breastbone, its ornate golden dragon head and sharp winged quillons all but hidden under the draped ivy and creeping moss which had grown undisturbed for two decades. Rúni gasped and tore his hand from hers, dashing forward to brush away the moss and run his hands over the shining hilt.

"Rúni!" She stretched out her arm, but there was no stopping him. His fingers flew over the carved dragon with childish reverence, but no lightning from heaven smote him for his audacity. He tightened his hand around the leather grip just above the gleaming dragon and tugged with all his might, but the hilt might as well have been carved from the stone and merely painted to look like a sword; it budged not even a hair's breadth.

The witch watched his fruitless efforts with amusement, slowly circling the massive stone. "I'd thought so often about hollowing it out," she reminisced, "just as I did with my tree, but it would be so much work. Then she returned the sword to its rest, so no rock house for me. Finndís, if you please?"

Finndís blinked at her. "Pardon?"

Eirný's lips twisted into a fresh smile as she shook her head in exasperation. "I could have sworn we agreed I was showing you your sword. Did I not say that? You *are* Ásdís' granddaughter. I can see her in your face, even had I not watched you in my dreams."

"I..." She felt Torjei at her back; her chest was too tight, her breath struggling in its rhythm. Each word felt like a stone disgorged from her throat, scratching her insides on the way up. "I *am* Ásdís' granddaughter. But that doesn't make the sword mine. It belongs to her heir, not to the first girl who comes along."

"Did you never imagine that might be you?" asked Eirný, watching her with bright birdlike eyes.

Finndís' gaze drew back to the golden hilt as she felt a flutter of need coil in her gut. Yes, she had imagined this. They'd played games as children, she and her two older siblings. Her brothers had spun elaborate scenarios to thwart the prophecy: the stone would shatter or dissolve or melt away so Leifur or Magni might wield the blade as king. But in her dreams at night, Finndís was the one who held the sword and not through any trickery; the blade leaped easily to her hand, undeniably hers by birthright.

Yet those were childish dreams. Every time she'd taken a step towards the western Witchwoods, she would remember her duty to her strict father, or her responsibility to keep Torjei safe, or a thousand other reasons why she ought not run into danger. She'd watched her brothers grow up, marry, and sire children, and she'd waited with trepidation while her own future was haggled over by others. If she had a great destiny, surely it would have manifested itself by now; if magic existed on her doorstep, it would have touched her mundane life in some way. No, she was no predestined queen; she was simply Finndís.

"Please, Finn?" Rúni crept back to them, picking his way around the mushrooms dotting the lush ground. He slipped his hand into hers and looked up at her with the expression which had wheedled so many treats from the castle kitchens. "Please try? It would be so amazing if you could do it! Think of coming home with Grandmother's magic sword! Wouldn't that make everyone happy?"

Not Father. Finndís bit her tongue to keep the words back from her little brother.

Yet while Rúni was an innocent, Torjei was not. Reaching out, he rested his hand on her shoulder. "Many people would be glad," he said, answering her unspoken objection. "This land longs for a queen." A cloud passed over his face, pained and selfish and fearful of change, and she understood his hesitation because it was written on her own heart. "But only if you *want* to be queen, Finndís."

She took a sharp breath at the sound of her name on his lips, letting the cool forest air slip into her throat. *Queen!* She could help people as queen; she could unite the tribes and beat back the brigands and bandits who preyed on the weak. She could be herself, too, and that was far from nothing. Whatever bindings were placed on her as queen, whatever oaths she must swear to her people, her name would be *hers*. No longer a cherished secret held close to her heart, others would use her name as Torjei had just now. 'Finndís the First', they would call her, granddaughter of Ásdís, great-granddaughter of Védís.

She exhaled again, the breath warm on her lips. "You know this is all for nothing if I'm not the right one," she muttered to Torjei, stepping forward to stand in the shadow of the stone. "We're going to feel silly if this doesn't work." Downcast, too, she knew. The hopes she'd buried long ago as a child in her father's court had awoken and now all she could do was grip them tightly and pray they didn't slip away.

Reaching out, she let her fingers slide over pebbled leather and smooth gold. Whichever smith had crafted the sword, they had created a work of art. A fraction of blade protruded from the stone, its edge untouched by time or rust. The powerful dragon head and wings forming the ornamental guard beguiled her eyes, and the wrapped leather hilt was soft as sheepskin under her touch. Beneath lay a thrum of magic, a primal sense of belonging. The sword was part of her, or perhaps she was part of the sword.

"My birthright." Her voice was a whisper as she let her hand tighten on the grip and gave a gentle pull, just as she would draw her knife from her belt; she felt a smooth sliding sensation. With a vague awareness that her feet were moving, she stepped back to make room as more of the blade appeared from within the stone sheath. Light gleamed from its naked surface, reflecting back so much more light than existed in the dark clearing. Finndís turned her head to follow the light and gasped when she glimpsed Eirný.

The witch's eyes were closed in rapture, her haggard face upturned to the trees with a smile on her lips. Around and above and through her flitted indistinct human forms. They were people of every shape and size: thick and thin, short and tall, lovely and ugly, but all of them insubstantial and ephemeral, clear as water in a cupped hand. Some seemed ancient, with bowed backs and wrinkles bearing witness to the dawn of time; others were infants, toddling with fat ethereal baby legs about the clearing. All were tied to Eirný with silver threads, the gleaming linkages draping her in a glowing gossamer net. Her body bathed the sword in light, and it reflected that light back upon her as she basked in glory.

With a final flash, the sword pulled free from its resting-place. Finndís clutched it close to her heart, both hands tight on the grip. Torjei held Rúni back as the boy stared open-mouthed, his head swiveling between the witch and his sister, unable to decide who was more fascinating. The ghosts, if that was what they were, faded as Eirný's light diminished. The witch's gaze meandered down from the trees to settle on Finndís and, though her face was still young, Finndís marveled at how very old her eyes now seemed.

"What once was has come into being again," Eirný whispered, her smile serene, "and you are all on the path to becoming what you shall be. Now it is time for you to return home. Follow me."

By the time they returned to the castle, the kitchen staff had given up waiting for fresh game and were busy putting together a dinner from the larder. Finndís' new sword, naked in her hands and ostentatious in its glory, raised every eyebrow they passed as the three walked from the castle stables to the great hall.

The doors to the great hall were open as they approached and heated discussion drifted down the stone passageways. Passion and drink made nobles loud, coupled with the confidence so many of them carried after years of being masters in their own castles. Finndís heard her brother's name over the clamor.

"Just because Magni has whelped an heir is no reason to hand him a crown! He can barely manage his own lands; I shudder to think what he'd do as regent!"

"At the bare minimum, he needs experience. If he could be persuaded to take on a small portion of the responsibilities of the crown as training—"

"Magni will never submit to sharing power with me, or with anyone else for that matter." King Njáll's voice was strong and stern, carrying over the others. "You who have met him know I am right in this."

"Nevertheless, we need a succession plan. As things stand, if something were to happen to you—I pray the gods perish the thought!—the kingdom would be torn between Leifur and Magni."

"It would be Sveinn and Orvar all over again, but without Ásdís to lead us."

"Lords, I still maintain that the prophesied daughter will come from *my* household, not those of my sons. I ask your patience for a little longer, as I—"

The gasp which rose from the assembled clan-lords cut short the king's words. He whirled to follow their gaze, his jaw dropping at the sight of his youngest children lingering in the doorway. Finndís stood front and center, the magical sword held in both her hands and resting lightly against her shoulder. Rúni trotted along beside her looking enormously pleased with himself, while Torjei stayed a few steps behind; present as he always was for her, but careful to convey his lower status with deferential body language when in public.

Finndís swallowed in the deafening silence. "My lords," she began, her voice dry but determined not to fail, "we return from the Witchwoods. I bear the blade of Queen Ásdís, my grandmother, as her granddaughter and heir." Blank faces stared at her and she took a deep breath. "Some of you know me but others I have not yet met. I am Finndís, daughter of King Njáll. I am honored to welcome you to our home."

Her father's face held a storm brewing, but it was old Lord Adils who spoke first. He was nobility by only the thinnest of threads: the father of Queen Ásdís' youngest sister, loyal to his queenly step-daughter, and elevated to nobility when one of her vassals had died without issue. However, he had become a lord before many of those present had been born and was like a grandfather to Finndís. His voice was a papery whisper in the quiet room, confused but not unkind. "Finn...dís? Weren't you a little boy? I remember holding you on my knee."

She shook her head, hands clutching the grip of her blade tightly for strength. "No, Lord Adils," she said, as gently as she could with her father glaring daggers at her; she would not let her voice quaver. "I have always been a girl. I told you this once, when I was very young; you might not remember."

His ancient face creased in a frown but he nodded slowly. "I do. I asked what a little boy might want for Candletide. You corrected me." His chuckle was warm as rich liquor. "I had quite forgotten."

The other clan-lords were less amused, already gathering their wits and objections. "This is an outrage," sputtered a thin lord whose name Finndís did not know. His eyes raged like the sea over his sable beard. "If you had a daughter all this time, you ought to have told us so." He eyed Finndís with misgiving, suspecting trickery, but the gleaming sword in her hands was not counterfeit; she held the golden sword each lord present had longed to see in the hands of an heir before they died.

"Njáll, you pretended she was a boy? To protect her from threats as a child?" Finndís turned to find Lord Salbjorn watching her with a thoughtful gaze. She liked Salbjorn from what little she knew of him; he had a son her age who rarely attended court, being apparently too sickly to travel far from home. The defense he now offered Njáll was so opportune that she wondered if he had practiced the line and why; not at Njáll's request, she was sure. She made a mental note to meet later with Salbjorn and his reclusive heir, who might have more in common with Finndís than she'd ever before dared to dream.

Yet her heart sank when she looked at her father, recognizing anger simmering just beneath the surface. This was the best solution he could have imagined; he would be father to a queen, not an elderly regent displaced by one of his ambitious sons or clinging to scraps of power while he rushed to sire more children. He was too stubborn to appreciate what was offered, unable to see past his public humiliation.

Finndís decided she would save him, though he did not deserve her help. She would save him because she loved him in spite of his faults, and because preserving his face before the lords would benefit them all. "He did, my lord," she answered Salbjorn in her firmest voice, looking him in the eye. "He hid my true identity in order to keep me safe. If you examine your hearts, you will see this was the wisest course."

The others murmured, but Salbjorn continued to rise in her estimation by accepting this with a thoughtful nod. "He could not have known you were the prophesied daughter," he pointed out, his voice pitched to raise over the murmur. "Any granddaughter of Ásdís was eligible, after all, and

101

there would be considerable danger to a young heir-apparent. King Njáll ably protected you from attempts to kill you or carry you off."

She matched his nod, not allowing the relief she felt to show on her face. "Precisely, my lord. He raised me in secret so that I remained safe and hidden until this day. But he has provided for me the best of tutors and his own excellent guidance." She glanced again at her father, gratified to see his mind working as she spoke. "He has trained me well."

The lords looked at Father, their previous outrage beginning to thaw. Finndís knew they resented being deprived of the opportunity to wheedle and ingratiate themselves with her as a child, but they would fall in line now because they must. If they did not someone else would, and they were well aware of that. She caught her father's eye and chose her words with care. "He still has much to teach me, but I am now ready to take my rightful place according to the prophecy and unite our people under a single banner of protection and peace."

Father met her gaze and she saw defeat steal over his face and drain away the taut anger. Finndís held the sword, after all. He could wait for sages and wand-wives to pronounce over her with their second sight, but to do so would undermine his own authority. Better to be the canny King Njáll who wisely raised a queen in secret and brought her forward in triumph than to be a fool who knew not the value of his own children.

He scanned the faces of the lords at the table, his expression stern once more. "I have always insisted that the daughter of prophecy would come from my household," he pointed out, his tone verging on the righteous scolding she knew he so dearly loved. "My lords, did you think this was an idle boast? I present to you now my daughter Finndís, your true and rightful queen. You have been brought here to plan her coronation."

As the lords burst into a fresh argument on the whens and hows of the ceremony, Rúni looked up and tugged on her sleeve. "Does that mean we get treats?" he whispered, beaming happily at the prospect.

She felt Torjei's hand on her back, steadying her now that the ordeal had passed and her knees were weak with relief. Looking at her companion, she raised an eyebrow and tried to hold back the silly smile spreading over her face. "Torjei, do *you* think Rúni should have treats?"

Torjei's own smile was radiant. "I obey my queen's every order, as you know," he murmured, lips twitching with mischief. "I will most happily follow her and her little brother to raid the kitchens. We can let them argue until they're exhausted, then you can sweep in with your decisions already made."

"Armory first," Finndís decided with a smile, relaxing into his hand. "I need a scabbard for my sword. Then food, then decisions; one of which is confining Rúni to his room before he can slip out again." Grinning, she led the way over the protests of her brother and the laughter of her companion and friend.

EARLY TO RISE

Content Note: Magical Curses, Non-Consensual Kissing, mention of Self-Harm

No birth is a small thing to the people involved, but the arrival of a long-awaited heir to good King Juste and fair Queen Osanne was a momentous state occasion which encompassed the entire kingdom. Bells tolled in churches and wine ran freely in public fountains throughout the land. Nobles dressed in their finest clothes and rode to the capital, tossing coins to the crowds lining the roads. People cheered as they passed, aprons outstretched to catch the glittering offerings. Official celebrations spanned more days than a week could contain and the jousts, dances, and feasts continued into the nights and spilled over into holy days. No one could contain their joy over the birth of little Princess Claude.

Days of celebration culminated in a great public presentation in which the princess would be shown to her people. Guests arrived from all over the kingdom for the event, as did representatives from other lands. Ambassadors brought gifts for the princess: rich clothes for her layette and beautifully-wrought toys; kings from foreign lands sent nobles hinting at their willingness to engage in marriage negotiations. Last to arrive but foremost among the guests were the nonhuman visitors who graced the court with their presence.

Three powerful fairies arrived in glittering pomp, displaying invitations at the door and basking in the awe of the crowd. Each lady represented both herself and the fae races she associated with, acting as ambassador to the humans on the part of those who could not attend the event. Lady Honoré swept into the great hall, dressed in rich red cloth folded to resemble fiery roses blazing in the torchlight. She hailed from the north and represented dragons, salamanders, will-o'-wisps, and other fierce and flaming dancers of the sky. Holding the baby to her breast, she pressed scarlet lips to the infant's forehead as the child cooed, promising a gift of creativity: Princess Claude would excel at every activity, guided by a passionate heart and vibrant mind.

In the wake of the fire fairy came Lady Désirée, in a gown which flowed like water studded with golden lilies. She had traveled far from the south and was patroness to the selkies and nixies, the water-dwellers who lived and moved in the deep rivers and wells of the kingdom. She lifted the royal infant high in her arms, smiling a tender smile, and laughed when tiny seeking hands caught at her hair and found flowing water where blue-green tresses seemed to tumble. Désirée promised the little baby a gift of grace: Princess Claude would move with beauty, her hands and feet touched with finesse. Whether dancing or fighting, running or gamboling, the child would move with fluidity, charming all who beheld these feats.

The third and final fairy stepped forward; this was Lady Giselle of the eastern woods, friend to brownies, gnomes, dryads, and forest people. Yet a cold wind whipped through the hall, chilling all present and extinguishing the merry torches dotting the stone walls. The swirling maelstrom gathered in the center of the room, winds whipping hard enough to slash anyone who stepped close, before coalescing into a fairy woman decked in feathers of every possible length, texture, and color. Lady Mélisande of the west— queen of chaos and wild things, patroness to airy creatures: birds, bats, and banshees alike—stood wrapped in her riotous rainbow dress and considered the gathered assembly with a cold, regal gaze.

"King Juste and Queen Osanne." Her eyes found the royal parents at the front of the hall and she addressed them with a tight little nod of the head, her voice cold as mountain snow. "What a magnificent celebration for such a momentous occasion: the birth of an heir." Her eyes fell on the golden cradle shrouded in fine silks. "I was quite surprised not to receive an invitation to the event."

King Juste quailed, knowing the danger of offending any of the fae race. "Lady Mélisande, your invitation was sent but did not reach you; our messenger believed that you had left our realm. Please forgive us."

The feather-clad fairy watched him with dark eyes. The chilly breezes which whipped about her ruffled the edges of her dress and surrounded her with quivering energy though she stood as still as the statues lining the hall. "One might accuse your messenger of giving up too easily," she mused, her gaze hard.

"Or one could take a hint and see that one was not wanted," Giselle tittered behind her hand. The little brownies and gnomes of the forest are fond of such jokes and put no stock in them, but Mélisande drew herself up taller and all breath left the room as the people stilled in alarm.

Queen Osanne broke the dangerous silence, worry for her newborn etched on her lovely face. "We are grateful to have you here now, Lady Mélisande. Please make yourself at home and feast with us. A place of honor will be set for you at our table." Her offer might have been enough, but for another giggle from Lady Giselle.

The fairy narrowed her eyes and a smile spread over her face. "You are very gracious, Queen Osanne, but I shall not tarry. Before I go, I too wish to bestow a gift on the child." The queen took a step towards the cradle in alarm but the fairy and her winds were already there, beating back all who would approach. The fair woman stooped to gather the baby in her feathery arms and studied her with grave intent.

"The princess shall indeed grow in skill and grace, the fairest of all in the realm," the lady announced, turning to present the child to the crowd as though she herself were the mother. "However, before the sun sets on her seventeenth birthday, she will prick her finger with a spindle and she shall die."

"No!" Queen Osanne hurried forward, one arm thrown over her face as she fought the buffeting winds. With a flash of light and the scent of candle wax on a winter's eve, Mélisande vanished and the child was left in her mother's arms; unharmed, but wailing in vexation at finding the pretty feathers taken away.

Guests wailed along with the infant and the king yelled for his guards, but the chaos was to no avail. No one knew where the fairy Mélisande made her home, nor could they imagine any threat or bribe that would make her reverse the curse she had laid upon the princess. When the king slumped defeated onto his throne, the last of the fairies stepped forward: young Lady Giselle, now chastened by her part in the affair.

"Your Majesties, do not grieve your daughter's death before her time," she urged, her soft voice like the merry jingle of bells. "I cannot undo Mélisande's magic, but I can alter the course it will take. The princess shall indeed prick her finger with a spindle, but she shall not die. She shall fall into a deep sleep, and the kingdom with her. Her sleep will last until she is awakened by true love's kiss, and then all shall be restored."

This last gift bestowed, the fairies withdrew from the hall and the humans were left to mourn when they had hoped to make merry.

"If we held a ball for Séraphine's birthday, we could invite Prince Régis. What do you think, dear?"

Claude kept her eyes on her painting, though she had to take the brush from between her teeth in order to answer. "Isn't he too old for her? She's only nine."

Osanne never sighed or groaned—to do so would be unqueenly—but the little pauses in her speech could convey a world of meaning. "You would be there too, Claude."

Now she did look up, feeling her entire body contort in a wince. "*Me?* Mother, I don't like Régis! He chews with his mouth open and his breath smells like cabbage."

Her mother lifted an arch eyebrow. "He is a high-spirited boy who likes to talk during dinner and enjoys his vegetables. If a man's table manners are his worst quality, those can be fixed with time and patience."

Claude let her lips twist into an expression which could be read as defeat or defiance depending on her mother's mood and turned back to her painting. The mixture for the sky wasn't quite right and this frustrated her; blue paints were the hardest to procure and finding exactly the right hue was time-consuming and wasteful. This particular piece had frustrated her almost beyond bearing and she was tempted to consign the entire canvas to the fireplace but didn't want to let it beat her. She would win.

If her mother would just leave her alone.

"We could invite Yves as well. You like him, remember? He has that lovely little duchy with the lake you enjoyed so much as a child. Remember how your father and I used to take you there?"

She tried to smile but the effort left her grimacing at the canvas. "Twice, mother. Yes, I remember." That seemed insufficient, so Claude searched for something more to say. "It was a very nice lake; peaceful."

"And Yves is a very nice peaceful boy, so that works out well," Osanne observed in her crisp manner. "I'll put him on the invitation list, along with Prince Régis. Is there anyone else you'd like to suggest?"

Claude felt her mother's eyes watching her, tension in the air as she waited for her to show some semblance of interest. Osanne didn't wish to make the conversation awkward—indeed, much of her role as a queen was to defuse tense situations, not exacerbate them—but on this one subject it was impossible for her to step back and give her daughter breathing-room. Claude swallowed the lump in her throat and spoke.

"Léandre?"

She felt her mother's hesitation in the tiny pause that followed. Léandre was neither prince nor duke, just the son of an earl. But he was gentle and lovely, with hair that flowed over his shoulders like spun gold, and half the girls in the kingdom wanted him. Osanne was in no position to be choosy so she put on her warmest smile. "Of course. I'll put him at the very top of the list. See you at dinner, dear."

"Mother!" Claude whipped around before she could retreat. "Do you like my painting? It's not quite finished yet and I'm not happy with the sky, but I think the trees along the bottom came out really well."

A long pause, gentle in intent if not delivery, conveyed all the sighs the Queen never breathed. "It's lovely, dear, as is everything you do. Please don't be late to dinner; it worries your father when you are." Osanne swept out, her skirts rustling against the floor like a soft breeze through autumn leaves.

"She never even asked if I wanted a party," grumbled Séraphine, glaring out through the glass pane to the courtyard below. Her knees were drawn up to her chest and her back rested against the stone behind her. The window seat was her favorite perch in the tower, and she often kept Claude company when she painted.

Claude formed her mouth into a sympathetic grimace, though she wasn't sure if the sentiment reached her eyes. "It's tough being the youngest," she offered, the words an olive branch. She wanted a royal ball even less than Séraphine did, but Séraphine was right: the celebration was being arranged on Claude's behalf, not hers.

"What would *you* know about it?" Séraphine was blunt to a fault. "You've never been the youngest. You were an only child until Valéry came along, and then you were the eldest. I've been the youngest since I was born. What are you painting? Giving up landscapes and moving on to castle scenes now?"

Claude blinked at the sudden change of subject and looked back at her canvas. Gray stone walls, open to the viewer, framed the lush frills of an enormous bed with billowing curtains pulled back just enough to show the hands folded modestly over the sleeper's chest. Roses in bloom filled the chamber; red flowers, because her instructors insisted love was that shade. Claude couldn't say if they were right but took their word as law.

"It's a painting of the... the situation. So that the prince will know what to do; or the duke or earl or whoever."

"'Whoever'?" Séraphine repeated with a snort. "Listen to you! Don't tell Maman you're pining for a stable boy. She's having enough trouble accepting an earl. But why wouldn't he know what to do, Claudie? The whole kingdom knows, along with everyone in the neighboring kingdoms. Traveling bards sing about the curse!"

Claude opened her mouth then closed it again; turning back to her paints, she set about the process of packing away her supplies. The canvas needed time to set before she could layer more paint into place. "Well, it's just in case," she said, choosing her words slowly and trying not to sound defensive. She didn't like talking about the curse—she couldn't get away from it for even a moment—but Séraphine didn't count the way others did. "Maybe he won't turn up for a long time, and people won't remember. If I have paintings up to explain the situation then he'll know what to do, even if it's a thousand years later."

"A thousand years?" Séraphine's mouth dropped open as she stared at Claude from the window seat. "Are you serious? Maman is expecting it to be a few weeks at the most. Why do you think she's so obsessed with finding the right boy for you to meet and fall in love with?"

Claude shook her head, not wanting to be drawn into that line of speculation; no one wanted to hear her say she had no idea what the 'right boy' would be, nor if she could ever feel the way they wanted her to feel. "I know, Séra. I know. But it's sensible to make plans. What if the first one dies on his way here? We'd have to wait for another True Love to appear. That could take a long time." *Or forever,* she added mentally.

"You're so morbid, Claudie." Séraphine unfolded herself from her seat and moseyed her way over to peer at the canvas, her nose inches from the damp paint. "I remember those clay sculptures you used to make of yourself sleeping; so still and solid, as if you were dead instead of asleep."

Claude sniffed, putting on her haughty artist's voice. "I was expressing myself."

"My point exactly." Séraphine laughed, turning on her heel; her dark eyes glinted and Claude wondered just how much she saw. Young as she was, Séra seemed the most mature of the three royal children, as though an old soul had bonded with the child in infancy. "Speaking of which," she said, her hand darting into the sash at her waist, "I found what you asked for, so you can 'express yourself' better on your next boy-day."

Silver glinted in watery sunlight that filtered in through the tower windows. Claude's breath caught and she reached with infinite care to touch the scissors. Sharp treasures were precious and rare in her world, given her parents' fears about the pricking of fingers. Scissors weren't a spindle on a spinning wheel, but Osanne and Juste were taking no chances with their children. "Thank you," she breathed, glancing at her sister as she tucked away the gift at her waist. "You know, you and Valéry are the only ones who believe me."

Séraphine smirked at her and tossed her long dark hair over her shoulder as she turned to leave. "Not quite the only ones. Be careful; you didn't get those from me, Claudie."

"Why do *I* have to be here for this?" Valéry groaned and leaned forward on the stool Claude had set out for him. The boy was older than Séraphine by a good two years, but no one would know it to look at them; Val continually squirmed and fretted like a baby hound aching to dash off after the latest sight or scent.

"Because I like the way the barbers do your hair and I need a model,"

Claude explained again, trying to maintain a patient tone. They looked at themself in the mirror, pulled up another long strand of hair, held their breath, and tried to bring the scissors in at precisely the right angle. There was a long pause as they held still, eyes narrowed at the mirror to be sure, then the satisfying whisper of hair being sheared.

The lock coiled on the floor like a black snake, poised to slither to safety now that it had been freed. Claude grinned and shook their head; already they felt lighter, as if they could float away on a cloud. Another long strand of glossy hair was divided and held out, another whisper of the scissors. Soft bangs in front tapering to jagged daggers jutting down between ear and cheek, a gentle feathery profusion of hair at the crown, and airy layers down the neck with nothing past the nape: that was what Claude longed for.

"Maman is going to be angry," Valéry warned, watching his sibling work. He squirmed again, twisting in his seat when Claude reached to measure his hair with their hands. "Where did you get the scissors?"

"That's for me to know," they said absently, mind on the task at hand. "Stop worrying. She won't be angry with *you*, Val. If you don't say anything she won't even know you were involved. It's not like you're the only boy in the kingdom wearing your hair in this style."

"But you'll be the only girl," he pointed out.

They turned back to the mirror, working more slowly now that they were at the nape of the neck. "Mmm. I doubt that's true, but even if it were, I'm not doing this for my girl-days; I'm doing it for my boy-days."

Valéry peered up at them, curiosity in his eyes. "What's today? Usually I can tell, but today I can't."

Claude glanced back at him, smiling in spite of themself. "Today is an 'ask me later' day, I suppose; I'm not sure myself. I've been in a bit of a mood this last week, but I'm fine, really. Just tired."

He made a face, slumping in his seat and resting his chin on his fist. "It's all the ball planning. Maman wants to have me measured for a new suit just for the occasion. I don't know why I have to attend. The whole point is for you to find a True Love, isn't it? Séraphine said so and no one denied it."

Claude gave him a sharp look in the mirror. "When did Séraphine say so?"

"In the kitchens earlier," Valéry said, sounding bored. "She and I went down there to sneak a bite to eat and they were talking about menus. Séra was in a mood. The cooks overheard her but no one said she was wrong."

Claude sighed and turned back to the task at hand, not wanting to let anything ruin their enjoyment of the moment. They were so close, just a few more snips. *There!* Claude turned in place, looking behind themself at the mirror to see the back and running a hand through the soft fluff at their neck. *Perfect.*

"She's not wrong," they admitted, turning back to Valéry. "Maybe we can still have fun, though, doing our hair and dressing up. Speaking of which, how do I look?"

He studied them with his soft baby-brown eyes, so much lighter than Séraphine's and Claude's dark eyes; he had taken after their father in every way. "I like it," he decided. "Do you think the True Loves will?"

Claude hesitated as they bent to sweep the hair clippings up with their hands. "Well, someone wouldn't be my True Love if they were discouraged by my hairstyle, right?" they pointed out, though they could hear the doubt in their voice. Claude had no experience with romantic love, but if it resembled the bards' songs of famous love affairs, they couldn't imagine hair getting in the way of someone's feelings.

Valéry considered this. "No, I suppose not." A pause ensued as Claude tidied up and Val thought his thoughts; Valéry wasn't someone who could be rushed when he was thinking. "Claude?"

They didn't look up, giving him space. "Hmm?"

"You don't have a True Love yet, do you?" He bit his lip while Claude hesitated and shook their head. "I didn't think so. Do you think you will in time for the curse?"

Claude didn't say anything for a moment, leaning back on their heels to take a deep breath. "Val, I don't know," they admitted, their voice low. "But please don't repeat this to anyone, not even Séra."

"I won't!" He bristled at the warning. "I'm not a baby, Claude. Anyway, we're brothers and brothers keep each other's secrets. Everyone knows that!"

Their face split in a grin. "Good point. We are and we do; brothers don't ever tell on each other."

He met their smile with one of his own, relaxing in his seat. "You're trying, though. Right? No one wants to sleep forever and people are worried. Séra says the whole thing is giving Maman white hairs."

Claude's breath caught in their throat and they nodded reflexively, a thoughtless automatic agreement. "Of course I'm trying. We still have time, Val. That's why the ball is so important to everyone. I'll fall in love and whoever it is will break the curse. We won't sleep more than a week at the most; you'll see." They forced a smile but it felt like the rictus grin of a skeleton. "It'll be like a relaxing vacation."

Valéry hopped down from his stool with an easy laugh, avoiding the last few strands of hair which littered the bedroom floor. "A week or so would be fine, I guess. Any longer would be awful; think how weird it would be to wake up when all that time had passed. Remember not to tell on me when Maman sees your hair!"

Claude wondered if there were anything more torturous than a ball no one wished to attend. A short list of activities presented themselves, of course, several involving angry wild animals, but she was fairly certain no one would expect her to enjoy those, nor would canapés be served to her in the process.

She felt sorry for herself, but the larger share of her pity was reserved for her mother. Queen Osanne sat at the head of the room alongside King

114

Juste in perfect regal dignity. Every line of her expression was controlled with iron discipline, but Claude could sense her disappointment. To have spent weeks and a hefty portion of the castle treasury arranging this ball, only to achieve this anticlimax must pain her.

Prince Régis was having a lovely time, to be sure, but not with Princess Claude. He'd spent the evening in the arms of Lady Éliane: twenty-two to his eighteen, devastatingly charming, and bearer of her family's ambition to be lifted from the lower ranks of impoverished gentry. Claude watched her dazzling smile in the candlelight and felt no ill will. Osanne must be furious, since despite being ostensibly a celebration of Séraphine's tenth birthday, the matchmaking intentions behind the ball were transparently obvious and for the good of the whole kingdom. But Claude was not annoyed; she wished Lady Éliane the best of luck.

Nor was the outlook any rosier with Yves. The young duke had ensconced himself in the company of half a dozen other boys his age, lounging together against the eastern wall of the ballroom. They were drinking, laughing, talking, and catching up after having been apart from each other since the last celebration—and doing everything in their power to ignore the pointed looks of their mothers who motioned in vain for them to join the dancing. Claude watched the group as she moved about the room, envying them. She liked the idea of boys she could spend time with, unburdened by the need to fall in love before it became too late.

Of the short list of hopefuls, Léandre had been the only one who came close to pleasing her. The two of them danced together five times, a number which would verge on scandalous for any other young woman in the kingdom. As her seventeenth birthday loomed in a few short months, people were growing desperate; if a pretty earl from the unfashionable end of the kingdom could charm the cursed princess with his soft gray eyes and flowing hair, then so be it. By their fourth dance, Queen Osanne watched with hope in her motherly gaze; during the fifth, Claude fancied that her mother was holding her breath.

Did she love Léandre? Claude couldn't be sure, but she didn't think so. Love was supposed to be a special thing, a magical feeling you knew in your heart. She'd waited all her life for it to strike, the way lightning struck trees during summer storms, but hadn't ever felt anything like it. She didn't feel it now. Léandre was beautiful, his hands were warm on her back, and his conversation was witty, polite, and respectful. He came from a good family who knew their place in the swirl of courtly politics, and if she were to marry him both he and they would be loyal to her till death. He would make an excellent prince consort.

Moreover, Claude liked him. She saw how hard he worked to make this work, the effort put into seeming effortless. He was an artist in his own way, sculpting himself for her and her parents and their people, creating beauty with the raw materials nature had given him. She wanted very much to be his friend, to steal away from the prying eyes of the court and just talk to him as an equal. Would they have anything in common, he and she? Claude imagined they might. They both lived public lives struggling to please their families and serve the common good. She wondered, too, whether he liked to paint.

But what she felt wasn't love; it wasn't romantic. She could like him, she could trust him, she could imagine doing her royal duty and marrying him, but she couldn't force herself to love him. And if she couldn't love him then Claude doubted she could make herself love anyone, for she wasn't likely to find a more attractive and amiable candidate than the young earl. After their fifth dance she excused herself and retreated to her rooms, telling Maman she needed to use the toilet. Queen Osanne was too pleased to object.

Claude wandered up the tower steps, taking her time and trying to erase the ball from her mind. It was all so much pressure: eyes watching her from every corner, waiting for her to find the right person, holding a collective breath for proof that she wasn't broken, that they wouldn't sleep for eternity because of a perceived flaw in her nature. Claude didn't *feel* broken; she *liked* the way she was. She didn't need romance to paint a sunset or dance a jig or sculpt a delicate rose from solid stone. People spoke of being completed by love, but Claude already felt complete. She was complete on girl-days, and he was complete on boy-days, and they were complete on the in-between days. Claude's life was full enough without True Love.

Yet that was a problem for everyone else.

She pressed open the door to her suite of rooms and was surprised to hear a rhythmic whispering noise, like the brush of silk against stone but over and over in a loop. Stepping silently on the balls of her dancing slippers, Claude followed the noise to the receiving chamber just outside her bedroom. There, in one of the chairs lining the curved tower walls, sat a little old serving woman doing something with her hands. Claude wasn't sure what she was about, more concerned with the presence of the woman than with her activity.

"Grand-mèrc?" Claude pitched her voice low and courteous, not wanting to startle the woman. She didn't recognize her, which meant the woman was not one of her or Séraphine's attendants. She might be one of her mother's vast army of attendants, but it seemed more likely that she was one of the ground-floor servants. Either way she should not be here in Claude's chambers, and certainly not alone.

"Yes, dear?" The woman flashed a toothy grin but kept her eyes on her work. A little bowl sat on her skirt between her knees. A long wooden stick, fat and round at the bottom and thin and pointed at the tip, like a child's spinning top, rested with the fat end in the bowl and spun around; the old woman's fingers kept the stick rotating with quick, constant movements at the pointed tip. All the while, she fed the stick from a cloud of wool in her other hand, creating spun thread that wound round the spinning wood. "Can I help you, child?"

Claude blinked at her, surprised at not being recognized. The old woman was clearly very confused. Servants were not supposed to wander into the crown princess' rooms, but she seemed harmless and was surely hurting no one by being here. Claude could leave her to work until the attendants came up after the ball. They would know who the woman was and where she ought to be sent for care. She peered at the stick in the woman's hands, intrigued by the rapid little movements of her fingers at the tip; the woman's hands moved so fast Claude could barely follow them. "What do you have there, grand-mère?"

"This?" The elderly woman laughed as though she'd asked a silly question, and perhaps she had; there was so much from which Claude was sheltered as a princess. "I'm spinning, dear. Yarn from wool."

"*Spinning?*" Claude recoiled, taking a step back and hearing her gown swish against the floor. The word had been drilled into her with horror almost from birth, a thing to be avoided at all costs. Yet she had seen drawings of the device she must always avoid, and this was no spinning wheel, nor was today her seventeenth birthday. The woman continued her work, oblivious to Claude's panic, and the fear in her pounding heart subsided until she felt faintly foolish. This woman and her little tool were no threat.

She stepped closer, feeling ashamed of her reaction. "Is it a new way of making yarn?" She'd never been able to immerse herself in yarn-crafts, frustrated by the lack of ready materials; she could, at a pinch, mix her own paints and plasters, but yarn had to be imported through complicated arrangements with foreign merchants.

"Eh?" The woman blinked at her and frowned, her fingers continuing to work. "I don't know if you would call it a new way; it's how my mother taught me, and her mother before. Would you like me to teach you, child?"

Claude hesitated. They were expecting her back downstairs at the ball, so she couldn't stay long, but she could spare a few moments. She reached for the little spinning stick, her smile rueful. "Yes, please, grand-mère, teach me. Oh!"

The tip of the stick spun to a fast blur, encouraged by the last twist of the old woman's fingers before she withdrew. Claude's hand was outstretched to take her place and she felt the bite of the spinning point. Blood welled up at the spot where her finger had been pricked and she saw a brief splash of red as the spinning stick flung three crimson drops across her floor, her painting, and her ballgown.

She leaped to her feet, stumbling back in panic, but already the world was spinning as rapidly as the little stick. A sound rose up around her, like the beating of a thousand wings, and she glimpsed a profusion of colors more wild and vibrant than her paints could ever capture. Faraway, as though in a dream, she heard a voice she must have known as a baby but had never heard again until this day.

"Before the sun sets on her seventeenth birthday, she will prick her finger with a spindle and she shall die."

Sunlight, bright and invasive, struck his eyes and he groaned. What time was it? It was rare for his attendants to let him sleep so late; usually he was up and dressed long before dawn. The cheery yellow light staining his bed and squeezing through the cracks of his eyes felt more like mid-morning. Was he ill?

Claude opened his eyes with some effort, bringing his hand up to his face to rub away the night-grit, but he stopped when he saw his sleeve. He was still wearing his gown from the ball. He lay in bed wearing an expensive gown that ought never to be worn in those conditions. Already he could feel the delicate fabric groaning as he used his elbows to push himself into a sitting position; if he moved any more, the lace in his sleeves would tear. Why wasn't he wearing his nightclothes? Where were his attendants?

Blood on stone, a tiny drip of dark red that none of his paints could ever perfectly capture, brought memories flooding back. A sharp little spindle spinning in a cup instead of on a wheel, and an elderly woman who wasn't what she seemed. But what did that mean? He waited, holding his breath to detect movement. The castle below his tower was impossibly still, a silence he'd not known even in the dead of night. His eyes darted around the room, but no one lurked in the corners or hid behind his easels. If he was awake, there ought to be a True Love who had performed the awakening, yet his room was empty. Who had kissed him?

Sun crept over the bedsheets, the deafening silence undisturbed except for the occasional flutter of wings as birds went about their business outside. Apparently nothing was going to happen unless Claude made it happen. Running his hand through his short hair, he hauled himself out of bed and then hesitated; he didn't want to traipse all over the castle in crushed velvet and thin dancing shoes. With some difficulty without his attendants, he stripped off his clothes and donned his best riding habit.

Feeling more like himself, and more comfortable in his boyish habit than in the frilly ballgown, he made his way down the tower steps. Here and there on the landings he found servants sprawled on the floor or sunk against the walls in sleep. The slow rise and fall of their chests as they barely breathed unsettled him. None of this made sense. If he was awake, everyone else should be too. Where was his True Love?

Hurrying past the trail of servants, he rushed to the feasting hall where the ball had been held. Claude's eyes widened when he entered the room. Everyone sat at their place, slumped over the table in sleep or leaning against the wall where they'd been standing. Séraphine lay in a nest of purple velvet and lace in the center of the dance floor, sleeping next to the boy who'd been her partner. Valéry had sunk under one of the tables, the pastry treat he'd been in the process of stealing still near his hand. King Juste and Queen Osanne sat in their matching thrones, leaning back against the plush fabric as they slept.

This was all horribly wrong. Claude was supposed to sleep, and the kingdom with her— him— *her*—

He stopped, his breathing turning shallow as his brain tried to sort through the tangle. What had the fairy from the eastern woods said? The words spoken over Claude's cradle had been drilled into him almost from birth. 'She shall fall into a deep sleep, and the kingdom with her.' Claude *had* fallen into a deep sleep on the evening of the ball, a girl-day. *She* had fallen asleep and the kingdom with *her*. Today, however many days later, Claude was a boy. This was one of his boy-days and he was awake.

That was it, then. He felt the blood drain from his face and he leaned against the wall before he could faint. There was no True Love to be found wandering the castle halls, because no one had kissed him awake. He had awoken because of a flaw in the curse, a mistake in wording. Instead of sleeping in stasis forever while awaiting a True Love, everyone else would sleep while he grew old looking for an answer to this problem. Would they sleep on forever after his death or would they die with him? He blinked as a new idea presented itself, harsh in the morning light: if he killed himself, would they then wake?

No, he couldn't think like that. There must be a solution he hadn't yet thought of.

Claude looked around the hall, running a hand up the back of his neck as he considered his options. Every eligible noble bachelor in the kingdom was here, which was an unexpected problem; the plan had been to send the most promising candidates out of the country for Claude's seventeenth birthday. After all, they couldn't kiss Claude awake if they were asleep themselves. He looked for Léandre and saw him slumped against the far wall beside his family; waiting for Claude to return, no doubt. Claude swallowed a lump in his throat.

Was it wrong to kiss someone while they slept? He hadn't thought much about it when he'd expected to be on the receiving end. But now that the situation was reversed, Claude felt distinctly uncomfortable at the idea of kissing a boy without his permission. Yet if the alternative was leaving everyone to languish in eternal sleep, he felt Léandre would understand. At the very least, if this worked and woke everyone then Claude would explain and apologize. If it *didn't*, well, he would cross that bridge when he came to it.

He took a deep breath and stepped over to the clump of bodies, picking his way around the sleepers on the floor. The silence was beginning to get to him; more than once he looked over his shoulder to confirm that no one had moved. Kneeling on the floor beside the young earl, Claude closed his eyes and prayed. *Let this work. Let me love him. I'll marry him and we'll have all the babies Maman could want; just let this work.* He puckered his lips and leaned over, brushing them against Léandre's mouth. Holding his breath, he waited.

Nothing stirred.

He pressed his fist into his mouth, stifling back a cry. He couldn't break down; sobbing would help no one. But if Léandre wasn't his True Love, who else was left to try? Claude felt even less for Régis and Yves; there was no point in working around the room kissing boys he knew for a fact he didn't love. Who was left? His eyes darted about the room, seeking a miracle or a sign of movement, and settled on the occupants of the thrones at the head of the hall: King Juste and Queen Osanne. *Papa and Maman.*

Claude knew without the slightest question that he loved them. Whatever his feelings about romantic love, whatever made him different from the star-crossed lovers in the bards' tales, he loved his family with all his being. Rising, he strode over to the thrones and stooped without hesitation to press a kiss to Maman's lips, the same kiss he'd given her every night of his life before his attendants bundled him off to bed: a kiss containing all the love he held in his heart for her. A kiss of truest, deepest, bestest love.

He waited with tears in his eyes for her to move. She slept on.

Kneeling beside her throne, Claude struggled to steady his breathing and remain calm. What had been the exact words of the curse? He closed his eyes and let his lips move through rote memory. 'Her sleep will last until she is awakened by true love's kiss, and then all shall be restored.'

Claude wasn't a she, and moreover he wasn't asleep and therefore couldn't be awakened. His problem wasn't that he didn't love Maman, but rather one of gender and sleeping arrangements: things over which he had no control. Claude felt a silent scream bubble in his throat. Was this his doom: to live out his life alone in a silent castle, everything around him unmoving?

No, not unmoving; he heard the flutter of wings again and the cry of a bird. The call crashed into the unnerving silence and he moved to the hall windows, seeking the sound. Pulling aside the curtains which had been drawn against the night, he was surprised when not an ounce of daylight filtered in.

"What is *that*?" His voice was loud in his own ears.

Sprawling hedges surrounded the hall, wrapping the castle in a protective barrier which extended as far as his eye could see in every direction. They rose to twice his height and were studded with thorns as long as his arm and as sharp as a blade, knit together so thickly that not a ray of light could pierce them.

Why would someone trap him here? Was this a fairy trick meant to keep his True Love out? Claude swallowed a bitter laugh. If that were the case, the joke was on them. No True Love was coming, nor was he in the proper state to receive one if they did come.

Claude had been raised to appreciate and understand pageantry, the ways in which elaborate ceremony stirs emotions in an audience. The part of him desperate to remain calm managed to be impressed as he stepped inside the long shadow cast by the hedge away from the rising sun. The massive wall of thorns probably didn't need to be well over twice his height but if the goal was to make him feel small and insignificant in comparison, then the gardener who had placed it here had done their job well.

He followed the length of it around the perimeter of the castle, careful not to stray too close to the thorns; visions of a stumble and headlong trip into their midst haunted him as he walked. The long thorns were sharp as rapiers, capable of blinding or even killing anyone foolish enough to wade into their midst. Moreover, the hedge was so deep that not a single stray sunbeam could pierce the tangled depths. Even if he could safely wade in, he couldn't imagine how far he'd need to penetrate before he came out the other side.

How had this grown? It had to be magic. He had no way of telling how long he'd slept, but even if he'd been asleep for years rather than the hours or days he suspected, there was no way this growth could be natural. Someone had shaped this hedge into a perfect oval around the castle, but *why* and *who* were questions to which Claude had no answer. Carefully he stepped closer and reached out to touch the hedge, only to yank his hand back when the tip of a thorn drew blood from his finger. He wasn't getting out this way.

Was that the intention, to trap him here? That made no sense; he wasn't supposed to be awake, so how could he try to leave? There was no sense in caging a person who was already trapped in slumber. Since the palace residents were similarly cursed to sleep until the arrival of True Love's kiss, the hedge couldn't be meant to keep them in either. Nothing in the castle stirred; even the horses in the stables were silent. Why was this barrier here, impossibly tall and impassably wide?

Perhaps he had it the wrong way round, thought Claude as he stepped back from the hedge and continued his circuit of the castle; maybe the barrier had been erected not to pen people in but to keep them out. Could the fairy who had cursed Claude at birth have gone further, actively trying to prevent any True Love from reaching him? Her task was superfluous, Claude was sure, but she had no way of knowing he didn't feel that way for anyone and didn't think he ever would.

He skirted the main stables, poking his head in briefly to confirm what he'd already guessed: horses slept comfortably in their stalls while the grooms who'd been tending to them snoozed in the straw nearby. A tabby cat, who held court over the stables and kept rats out of the hay, nested like a hen at the top of a shelf on the wall. Nothing stirred apart from the collective soft breath of so many bodies. Claude closed the doors gently behind him and turned back to the hedge, considering his options.

As long as the hedge stood, he was trapped. Maybe he could scrounge some of the ladders the servants used to clean windows in the great hall, and work out a way to strap them together to increase their length. Yet he'd cut himself to ribbons if he leaned the resulting ladder against the hedge, and even if he could successfully clamber to the top, then what? The hedge seemed as thick as it was tall; did he have the strength to haul up *more* ladders and set them horizontally across the top to walk over? More ladders would then have to follow so he could come down the other side. Claude doubted they owned enough.

Something nagged at him as he peered at the obstacle, and he chewed the inside of his cheek while he chased the thought. Hedges were a thing of earth, not air, yet the fairy who had cursed him was a patron of winds and birds. The one who saved his life, turning death into sleep at the cost of saddling him with the pressure of a True Love's kiss, had been a lady of earthy things, growth, and plants. Had she put the hedge here? He couldn't think why, unless it was meant as protection for the unconscious castle population against intruders. Perhaps the thorns would part for someone sufficiently pure in spirit.

If the hedge were the work of a benefactress, then its creator could be reasoned with if she returned. She must have visited the castle to grow the hedge, and someone had been inside his room; Claude had been in bed when he awoke, rather than sprawled on the floor where he'd fallen. If his guardian came back to check on things, he could explain the situation. Maybe she'd let him out of the hedge, and he could travel the world seeking to break the curse. Claude shook his head, feeling drained. The pressure to find a True Love had been almost unbearable; now the weight was crushing.

125

In the meantime, there was nothing he could do out here. Claude might as well go back inside the castle, though what he would do in there he wasn't sure. He didn't feel hungry, which he assumed was due to magic; at least he hoped so. How long would he have to wait for the earth fairy to return so that he could breach the hedge, assuming she returned at all? A thought struck him and he froze mid-stride: what if she returned on a girl-day? Would he fall asleep again when his next girl-day occurred?

Again he heard the flutter of wings and his head turned to follow the sound. He could hear no other movement than the wind; presumably any rats living in the walls now slept as deeply as the cats who hunted them. Why were the birds who fed on the orchards and nested in the towers not similarly asleep? He searched the sky for movement and his eyes widened when he saw an enormous riot of birds in every shape and size and color roosting on the western tower: the one they used for storage because it was too drafty to comfortably inhabit and no one wanted to sink money into renovating the ancient wing.

Claude hesitated on the castle steps, his heart beating fast. The birds who fluttered and flew above him went about their business, ignoring the human below. He'd never seen so many in one place, and half their number were unknown to him. One great scarlet bird was as bright as the sun at sunset; another with massive black wings and a ghostly white face seemed like death in avian form. They must have gathered here for a reason; something or someone must be inside the western tower, drawing these birds to itself. Claude took a deep breath and steadied himself against the stone wall. Maybe it was time to find answers.

She sat in the very center of the top room of the western tower, surrounded by birds and unaffected by the bitter wind whipping through the dusty garret. Her dress was a maelstrom of color and texture, boasting feathers as tiny as Claude's fingernails at the bodice and as long as his arms in the skirt. Her face was impossibly beautiful, fairer than any human could ever be; but when he cautiously climbed the tower stairs and poked his head into the garret, her expression was anything but lovely.

"You're awake?"

"I am." Claude offered her a deep bow. "Are you the great Lady Mélisande?"

Her eyebrows arched as a little red bird perched on her shoulder and chirruped loudly. "I am she," she agreed with a tilt of her head. "I had been led to believe that my name was out of favor in these parts."

Claude swallowed and wondered whether he dared lie; some said fairies could tell true words from false. "Madam, from my earliest days I have heard tales of your power. You are much respected in this land."

"You see?" Her lips curled into a smile, on the verge of a sneer when contrasted with her unfeasibly perfect face. "A reminder, now and then, helps people learn their place. Why *are* you awake? I did not expect it."

He hesitated, licking his dry lips as chilly drafts ruffled the feathers of her rainbow dress. "Madam, I confess I am not certain, but I believe I am awake because I am a boy today. Lady Giselle's, ah, gift of sleep was framed in terms which expected me to remain female for the duration."

Eyes as blue as the sky studied him and Claude thought he saw a flicker of interest. "You see how shoddy her work is," she complained, thinning her lips. "My curse was elegant. A youthful burst of grace and skill, cut away swiftly by death; the stuff of tragedy. No messy lingering in sleep until this or that event occurs; no gray area concerning what would happen if the subject's gender shifts like a wind current. Sloppy work. Amateurish, even. You ought to be offended to receive such a gift."

Claude took a deep breath, trying to channel his mother's patience. "I cannot argue with the truth of what you say, Lady Mélisande; your gift was far more direct. I'd hoped to find Lady Giselle and ask if she could undo her spell but as I find you here, could I beg *you* to be the one to lift her curse?"

He quavered to ask, for lifting the curse of sleep might bring about his death. Yet perhaps the mercurial fairy would forget that part or he might manage to avoid pricking his finger again before his birthday, for surely he could argue that his death ought to result as a direct consequence of the spindle-prick rather than hours or days later. If he must die, however, at least his family and people would be awake.

Her lips split in a wide grin and she screeched with glee. "Oh! Oh-ho-ho, no! Of course not. A fairy can't undo another's magic. If we could, Giselle would simply have undone my curse. Why do you think she altered its course instead? No, I cannot lift her curse; she has charged you all to sleep and sleep you shall."

Claude's heart plummeted. The request for Mélisande to lift the sleeping curse had been a long shot, but desperation had raised his hopes. He was no worse off than when he had entered the garret, but it felt as though he'd suffered a fresh blow. Struggling to steady his breathing, he decided he needed to get through the hedge barrier so he could look for an answer outside these walls.

"I did not know that, madam. Thank you for the information." Determined not to weep in front of this woman, he took another deep breath. "May I ask if you created the hedge around the castle? I need to pass through and I notice that you are here, unhindered by its presence."

Mélisande laughed again, a high little giggle. "I was already here. Remember the little old lady and her spindle? You should have seen your face! No, the hedge is earth magic, not mine. I assume Giselle put it up to screen candidates. Only True Loves allowed; can't have thieves running off with the silverware." She sniffed, amusement flickering over her unearthly face. "She didn't consider people who can fly. Her head is full of dirt! We noticed this nice garret and thought we'd make use of it; didn't we, pet?" she cooed at a falcon which had alighted on her wrist. "No, if you want the hedge taken down you'll have to ask Giselle."

"That's it, then?" The last of his hopes dashed, Claude felt a painful lump rise in his throat. "Everyone I care about is going to sleep forever while I'm stuck here waiting for the arrival of something that may not even exist? My True Love? But I don't *have* a True Love! I don't even *want* one!"

The fairy's eyes flashed with mischief and she grinned teeth as white as winter clouds. "Do you have any particular feelings for fairies? I haven't had a boy in a while, and you're cute. Perhaps you have been unnecessarily limiting yourself to humans. Experimentation could be pleasurable, and I *was* planning to stay here a while."

Claude blinked and waited for his heart to resume beating. He harbored a thousand objections to this idea but he must remain polite; he'd suffered through one lifetime already for discourtesy shown to this woman. "Lady Mélisande, I'm flattered but I don't know if True Love is something that exists for me. Certainly I cannot find it while under this curse, as my every interaction is tainted with enormous and unbearable pressure. I cannot make an attempt with you and must decline your kind offer."

"Mmm." She shrugged, looking bored as she gazed at the falcon. "Well, I suppose you'll have to find someone else then. Good luck."

"Could you fly me out on one of your birds, or send word to Giselle—?" Claude stopped and glanced at her with a frown as a thought occurred to him. "Forgive me, but you said Giselle *can* take down the hedge if she were so inclined?"

Mélisande nodded, looking up with a single raised eyebrow. "Well, yes, it's her own creation."

"Fairies can undo their *own* magic? Not each other's magic, but their own?"

"Of course! How else would magic work?"

"Lady Mélisande." He considered going down on bended knee, but he didn't like the idea of stepping closer to the falcon who was watching him with hungry eyes. "Will you please undo your curse on me?"

This produced a modicum of interest and she studied him with bright eyes. "What would be the point? You're not dead and I've done my trick with the spindle. Quite entertaining, wasn't it? I could have done it at any time, you know, but I waited until it would be most funny. Giselle isn't the only one with a sense of humor. Why would you want me to undo a curse which is already complete?"

"Because it's *not* complete," Claude urged, fighting an anxious impulse to chew the inside of his cheek. "Lady Mélisande, you said Giselle's curse—the sleeping, the true love, the hedge—altered the course of yours. If you undo your curse, the death curse that serves as the foundation for everything else, will hers crumble?"

She tilted her head for a moment, looking as much like a bird as the creature on her arm. "Possibly," she allowed, and Claude felt the air knock out of him in the sudden rush of relief. "But why should I?"

Throwing caution to the wind, he fell to his knees. "Lady, your curse served its purpose. My parents disrespected you, but because of what you did I was raised with the utmost respect for your name. This kingdom knows your power and the price of angering you. Yet if you leave us to rot like this, you will not be respected; you will be hated and denigrated. Your name will be dragged through the mud because of Giselle's foolish mistake. They will forget that the shoddy work was hers and will wrongly attribute this mess to you."

Her lips twitched, a gathering about the edges which spoke of old anger, deep and bitter. "They would not dare. Any fool who so slanders my name will be corrected. Painfully, if necessary."

"What if there were another way?" His heart pounded in his chest but he held her gaze. "You can undo the curse. I come humbly before you to beg your forgiveness. Judge for yourself that my family has learned our lesson, mended our ways, and will henceforth be your true friends. You are welcome at our court to forever sit as a guest at the highest place of honor. You can be my fairy godmother!"

She blinked at him, tilting her head so far he half-expected it might rotate like an owl's. "Your what?"

"My guardian. My *protector*. It is a great honor to be a godparent to royalty." He swallowed hard, wishing his throat were not quite so dry. "You would be seated at the head of our table at every event. If I marry or bear children, your presence would be expected at the ceremonies—if, ah, it suited your schedule, of course."

Mélisande studied him, her expression unreadable as a bird on her shoulder buried its beak into a wing to scratch at itself. "I keep my tower," she demanded, her feathery skirts shifting as she crossed her legs and settled deeper into her makeshift throne. "My birds have become quite fond of it."

"Of course." Maman would not be pleased to have a fairy in residence, but they would make it work.

"Are there any other fairy godmothers in the family? I wouldn't be sharing the title with someone else?"

He shook his head. "Not a single one. You would be the only one in the kingdom. A unique and honored guest at every royal occasion, immortalized in painting and sculpture throughout the land; my own paintings and sculptures among them, my lady. The other fairies gave me artistic talent, but I will use their gifts to honor you."

The birdlike fairy almost preened. "I've attended many a royal ball here before, you know. I danced with your great-grandparents, actually! Human favor is always so fickle, but I don't mind trying again; at least for a decade or two." She reached out a hand, her eyes flashing with fresh intrigue. "Deal?"

Claude's breath caught and he rose with care, stepping forward to take her hand in his own. This could be a trick, a trap, a cruel joke, but as they touched a sigh seemed to shudder through the castle. Through the tower window he saw the hedge crumble into dust, leaving only a soft circle of earth surrounding the castle. From below he heard movement, and his heart leaped with joy as a chorus of sleepy voices mumbled in confusion, demanding answers no one could provide.

"You did it," he breathed, grinning up at the fairy woman with unforced gratitude. "You broke the curse!"

Her smile was as beautiful as the day and a wild as an uncaged bird. "I told you I could. Now, my little godchild, let us go downstairs so that you can introduce me to your court. I have waited over sixteen years for a proper invitation, and I don't wish to wait another moment."

No Man of Woman Born

Content Note: Governmental Oppression, mention of Emergency Cesarean Births, mention of Rape

Neopronoun Pronunciation Key: Kie ("kee" or /ki:/), Kir ("keer" or /kir/)

The prophecy was very clear: 'No man of woman born can harm Fearghas.' It had been made by a somber and reputable druid, and confirmed by numerous witches and oracles throughout the kingdom. One or two of them could perhaps be suspected of spreading official propaganda out of fear or from motives of avarice, but they couldn't all be guilty of compromised integrity. No, the prophecy was unambiguous with independent verification from multiple magical sources.

Even if the prophecy had been official propaganda, it hadn't helped the king. Men still tried to harm him, though none succeeded, while others in the kingdom sought more creative ways to enact harm while satisfying the constraints of the prophecy. An underground industry sprang up almost overnight, determined to unseat the overlord whose reign brought misery to so many.

Schools were founded to teach women to fight, many headed by women as a precaution to ensure that any harm meted out by a student could not be indirectly attributed to a man. Other schools enrolled children in their

133

ranks, arguing that 'man' was something attained through age and maturity and not applicable at birth. Some aspiring heroes even went so far as to train animals, raising whole menageries of killer bears, dogs, and wild cats with the intention of mauling evil King Fearghas should the opportunity ever occur.

Innes was not a woman, a child, or a wild animal, but he scraped together all the money he could in order to attend a school run by a woman named Màiri. She was a glorious giant of a woman, taller than most of the men in town, and her scalp was shaved once a month to clear away the dark mossy stubble of her hair which never gave up growing. Màiri had lost her right leg in one of the border wars—Innes wasn't sure which one—and she walked with a cane and a wooden leg, a beautiful piece of carved hickory and metal, attached to her knee with leather straps.

Màiri's leg was the only reason she was willing to enroll Innes. Just past puberty, it seemed unlikely that he would not be a man soon, and Màiri didn't have time to waste on students unable to circumvent the prophecy. However, Innes' father, Eoghan, had lost his left arm in a bandit raid when he was just a boy and had been apprenticed to a blacksmith who had fitted him with a series of prosthetic arms as he grew. Now Eoghan made his own arms and was the best blacksmith for twenty leagues in any direction. He had made Màiri's leg, and Ainsley, Innes' mother, had tailored the straps which held the leg in place. Ainsley was as good a tailor as her husband was a blacksmith, and they both served the town residents well.

Innes' savings from making deliveries paid for his lessons, but it was his parents' reputations which got him through the door to Màiri's cellar and her secretive underground fighting classes. All the other students were viable candidates for subverting the prophecy: girls, women of all ages, a handful of very young boys, and two students around Innes' age who had explained to the class that they were neither girls nor boys. When he'd first signed up, Innes hadn't realized it was possible to be a gender other than the one you'd been assigned at birth, but the students seemed very certain and he accepted that they were in the best position to know. They certainly knew more about their own experiences than Innes did.

He couldn't say why it was so important to him that he train. Innes knew he was no grand 'chosen one', special from birth. His hatred of cruel King Fearghas was no deeper than anyone else's, and Innes had experienced less harm than most from the oppressive regime; no one in his immediate family had been taken away by the royal guard, just one cousin and a few childhood friends. His passion for justice was real, but he couldn't point at a defining moment which had solidified those feelings.

There was no doubt in his mind what his role would be in the coming revolution. If and when it came, his skills would be there to support the leaders. He wouldn't be at the front leading the charge, but he would be there all the same. If Innes couldn't harm King Fearghas, he could still take down any royal guards standing between the evil king and the chosen one. Until that day, Innes would train under Màiri's tutelage and learn everything she could teach him. He wouldn't fail her or the cause she worked for.

"Have you heard the latest prophecy?"

Sìne sat beside him on the low stone wall which kept Farmer Gillespie's sheep from losing themselves in the forest on the outskirts of town. Innes was panting heavily after their practice session, but Sìne seemed as cool as a spring breeze. She always did, really; she mastered every move Màiri taught them in half the time Innes took. He took another gulp from the jug he'd brought with him. "No; what was it about?"

She laughed, a sharp mirthless bark. "What are any of them about these days? King Fearghas, of course; how to kill him off once and for all. Hand that over, will you?"

Innes perked up as he handed her the jug. In a world of potential prophecy candidates, all of them 'no man of woman born', *how* to kill Fearghas had become the sticking point. If gossip from the capital could be believed, the last attempt on the overlord's life had involved an exotic undetectable poison, a goat, and a young culinary genius. The plot had failed to the detriment of everyone involved and the overlord still lived, though it was said he no longer enjoyed soft cheese.

"Does it give any clues as to how to do the deed?"

Sìne tilted back her head, hefting the jug high to coax out the last drop. "I wish! No, this one is more qualifications for would-be heroes. They're putting together a list of signs so they'll recognize the right one."

"More signs? Cutting out half the population in a single swoop wasn't enough?" Innes shook his head in exasperation at the unfathomable motivations of mages and took the empty jug back from her.

She laughed as she pulled her leg up on the wall for a post-practice stretch, leaning over to grab at her toes to keep her muscles loosened. "Well, there's the remainder to winnow down," she pointed out. "There are actually quite a few of us who aren't men born of women, Innes! It would be nice to know which of us is fated to kill Fearghas, so we can stop wasting time and effort on those who aren't."

His lips twisted into an annoyed pucker, but he couldn't argue with her logic. "Okay, what are the new qualifications? No woman born of man? Then we'd really be in a pickle."

Sìne snorted and gave him a playful shove on the shoulder. "Excuse me, but you're forgetting the neithers. Watch it or I'll tell Niven and Graeme; they can remind you of their existence on the training mats." She chuckled and began stretching her other leg. "No, the latest item on the checklist is two living parents."

Innes was surprised to feel his heart leap in his chest. He was already disqualified or soon would be; he couldn't dodge becoming a man forever. But here was a portion of the prophecy he could satisfy, even if he didn't meet the rest of the qualifications. He felt a strange sense of validation, even knowing this was foolish. The point of a prophetic checklist was to whittle away all those who didn't fit, in order to find the one solitary person who did. His partial compliance wasn't special; given a list long enough, the whole world would fit one piece or another. So why did his blood thrill with the knowledge that he met at least one small standard for heroism?

He tried to hide his elation, retreating to the safer territory of scholarly speculation. "I suppose that settles the question of whether battlefield-born infants are 'of woman born'?" Babies cut from their dying mother's wombs were the stuff of bards' tales in country inns, but Innes had never heard of any such thing actually happening. Still, storytellers loved the idea and worked it into their epic songs when given any excuse to do so.

Sìne shrugged and bent at the waist, gripping her toes with the tips of her fingers. "I suppose so, but it does disqualify a whole lot of the rest of us in the process."

The disappointment audible in her words shook Innes out of his own feelings and he winced. "Sìne, I'm so sorry! I hadn't thought about how that would affect you." Sìne's father had died in an attack on the town by the royal guard when she was only five years old; after that, her mother had raised her alone.

"Yeah, well." She shrugged, looking out over the sheep field with grim determination. "What can I do?"

The words weren't intended as a question but he echoed them back at her, watching her face intently. "What *are* you going to do? Drop out of Màiri's school?" Innes couldn't imagine class without Sìne; she was one of the best and most dedicated students, mastering each lesson with ease only to turn around and help the others.

Sìne took a deep breath and shook her head. "No. I'll stay on."

"But—"

She raised a hand to interrupt him. "Look, either I'm the hero or I'm not. If I am, this prophecy is wrong or there's something about myself I don't know. Maybe I have another father out there; perhaps my mother was sleeping with more than one man nine months before I was born and the one we thought of as my father wasn't really. Heck, I was conceived during a town occupation; my father could be a soldier for all I know."

Innes turned this over in his mind, his eyes wide. "Are you going to ask her?"

Sìne thinned her lips. "Would *you* ask your mother if she'd been raped and hadn't mentioned it to you?"

He blanched and looked away. "I guess not. But don't you care about the prophecy?"

"Of course I care." She hopped down from the wall and stretched one more time, looking off in the direction of the town. "I'm choosing to believe I have the capacity to become the hero until proven otherwise. C'mon, the sun's going down and I don't want to step in a dung heap in the dark."

"Do you think the prophecies are prescriptive or descriptive?"

Innes' question was punctuated by a thud as his arrow hit the target. Granted, not where he wanted on the target—the shaft was embedded a full handspan from the painted mark in the center of the target—but the arrow *had* hit the target and stayed there. He was improving.

"What do you mean?" Graeme stepped up to the line and took aim. Innes watched them draw their string back to the very tip of their nose and studied their positioning rather than the target Innes knew they would hit. Graeme was a natural with a bow and Innes was desperate to learn their secrets.

He waited until their arrow struck true, not quite at the center of the target but barely a hair's breadth away. "Well, when the mages say no man of woman born will kill Fearghas, and that the hero will have two living parents, and tomorrow they might say the hero will have a birthmark in
138

the shape of a dagger, do you think those are qualifications the hero has to actually have? Or do you think the mages look into the future to see who does the deed and they're just providing us with a description of that person?"

"Innes, do *you* have a birthmark in the shape of a dagger?" Niven was up next, kir lips twisted in a wry smirk as kie readied an arrow.

"A rabbit, actually," he was forced to admit. "At least, that's what my mother tells me; I can't see it myself without a mirror and serious neck strain. That's not the point, Niven."

"Is there a difference?" They both looked up at Graeme, who made a face at their matching expressions. "Not between a dagger and a rabbit, you big babies. Is there a difference between a predictive prophecy and a descriptive one? It's all the same to us at this point, isn't it? The hero must meet the prophesied qualifications because the hero *will* meet the qualifications."

Innes frowned as he worked through this line of reasoning. He liked Graeme; they hadn't been close enough in age to be playmates as children but growing up he'd thought of them as something like a cousin or distant big brother. Two years ago, Graeme had asked the town to use 'them' instead of 'him' for themself. Innes hardly ever messed up now, the new pronouns coming easily with practice. He didn't understand why Graeme wasn't a boy, but he recognized that he didn't need to understand a thing for it to be true.

"If the prophecies are providing details of a specific person, the way you'd describe someone you met in a village inn, then they could be changed." Innes found his hand moving in useless circles as he spoke; he grasped his bow with both hands to stop himself. "Fearghas could hunt down the hero and murder their parents, for example, now that he knows living parents are a prophetic marker. If he killed all the parents in the kingdom, would the prophecy become wrong? Would it be changed by events, the future altered by our response to it?"

Graeme gave him a look that was three parts exasperation and one part gentleness, the latter a recent addition in an attempt to improve their 'people skills'. "Innes, you can't change the future. Whatever they prophesy about the hero is true because it *will* be true. Fearghas could try to murder every parent in the land, but he would fail to kill the hero's parents; they'd be spirited away or hidden or otherwise saved. How can there be a difference between a description of what will come and a prescription of what must come?"

Innes felt there was a flaw in this somewhere, but Niven opened kir mouth before he could argue. "Here's what I want to know: does the hero actually *need* those bits and pieces in order to succeed? If the hero has to produce two living parents, do they help to kill Fearghas somehow? If the hero isn't a man, is that relevant in some way? We keep trying to work out how to do the job, but maybe the clues are in *who* can do it."

"Unless the prophecy is just a description!" Innes pounced on kir words. "That's exactly what I mean. Can *anyone* kill him and we're only hearing about the person who gets there first, or are the prophecy markers genuinely necessary qualities the hero needs in order to *be* the hero?"

"*Yes*," Graeme said, their voice firm and certain. "The prophecy descriptions must be met by the hero because they *will* be met by the hero."

"None of which answers my question," grumbled Niven, drawing kir bow and releasing a shaft straight into the tree trunk above the wooden target. Kie crowed with delight as kir arrow vibrated to a halt in the thick trunk. "Bullseye!"

Innes frowned at kir. "What are you talking about? You missed."

"Not at all; I hit the man's head, not his chest. Can we get Màiri to set the target higher, do you think?"

"Why are you so hung up on the prophecies?" Niven had stayed behind after practice to help Innes clean up. The king couldn't outlaw archery when so many people depended on the meat brought in by hunters, but it was wise not to draw attention to their training. The target was buried between practices, quietly covered over with earth and leaves, and the arrows plucked from the trees to be repurposed or disposed of.

Innes looked up from where he was trying and failing to wrest an arrow stuck fast in a nearby tree. "What? I'm not!" He narrowed his eyes at kir. "Anyway, you're as interested in them as I am."

"Because I think there could be clues in them," kie answered cheerfully, scooping up loose earth to scatter over the target. "If we piece together the puzzle, we'd know how to kill him. Apart from that, I don't care in the slightest what a bunch of mages say. I'm going to work out how to kill Fearghas and do it, and the rest of you can figure out how to apply the prophecies to me afterwards." Kie peered up at him. "But you've always got your ear to the ground for rumors of more predictions. Some days it's all you ever talk about. Why is that?"

The question made him pause. "Because I care! Finding the hero is very important, you know. I want to help them when they're found, so it's important to be well-versed on what qualifications we ought to be looking for. Educating myself is important if I want to be an ally to the hero."

"Uh-huh." Kie mounded the loose dirt to one side so kie could wedge the painted board in place. "Sounds to me more like you want to be the hero and you're looking for confirmation from someone else. Are you hoping for a prophecy that'll predict the hero will have a rabbit birthmark, eyes the color of acorns, and frizzy hair that goes wild when it rains?" Niven flashed him a warm smile. "Or that his name starts with 'I'?"

"No!" Innes shook his head but kie stared him down with dancing eyes; after a moment, Innes looked away. Niven hadn't known him from childhood the way Graeme had, being a more recent resident of the town, but kie had a way of reading his thoughts from his face. He wondered if kie saw the lie there and knew how gratified Innes would be if they came out with precisely those prophecies. Kir question echoed in his head: *Why?*

141

"It's not that I want to be the center of attention," he tried to explain, not meeting kir eyes. This was not a deliberate lie, but he struggled with whether or not it was strictly true. He *hoped* it was true, at least. "I don't need to be the hero. Someone else can be the hero, honestly! I just really want to help, and I feel a... a connection with the hero. I'd like to have similar attributes, even if I can't actually be the chosen one myself."

"Right." Niven stood, brushing kir hands on kir tunic to clear away the lingering soil. Kie gave him a sharp look. "Innes, maybe it's not my place to ask, but I'm going to anyway: are you a man?"

He'd heard the question before, of course; he was enrolled in Màiri's class and presented as masculine. Graeme was asked equally often, their reaction varying depending on the speaker, their tone, and how many times in a day they'd already had to answer the same question. Innes was never offended, but neither did he know how to respond. He stared at Niven and found himself shrugging his shoulders. "I suppose so?"

"Not a resounding 'yes', huh?" Kie leaned against a tree and peered at him with a skeptical gaze, soft at the edges. "I ask because, well, maybe you don't want the prophecies to fit you so much as you want yourself to fit the prophecies." Kie arched a thin eyebrow at him. "Innes, you do know you don't have to be a man, don't you? I mean, you've met Graeme."

"Well, of course I have." Innes felt defensive; he'd known Graeme longer than Niven had, after all.

Niven ignored the annoyance in his voice. "Have you ever thought you might be like them?"

Innes shrugged again. A part of him felt trapped by these questions, squirming and unable to flee; but a piece of his soul sang at being allowed to talk about it, at having a friend who looked at him and saw the indecision there. Someone who didn't judge him for not knowing. "I've thought about it. I... I *believe* Graeme when they say they're not a man? But I don't really understand why they aren't or how they can know. I mean." Innes laughed and tried to ignore the ragged edge to the sound. "Does anyone ever *feel* like a man?"

142

Kir eyebrow arched higher. "I suspect some men do, yeah."

Innes pursed his mouth, looking away again. "How did you know about yourself?" He'd first met kir when he joined Màiri's school; Niven had introduced kirself by name and pronouns. *'Kie' as in 'key' as in 'lock up your hearts',* kie'd said. *'Kir' as in 'peerless' as in 'better than you'.* Innes had been skeptical of that last part until kie proved it on the training mats with painful clarity.

Niven laughed, the sound a soft huff of air on the breeze. "How do you know when a shoe doesn't fit quite right? It covers your foot and it's better than nothing at all, because you're not getting burrs stuck in your heel when you walk, and no shoe is perfect. Maybe if you just wear thicker socks, it'll feel right. Maybe *all* shoes are bad and you just need to accept it and stop complaining that your feet hurt." Kie grinned, shaking kir head. "And then one day you take the shoe off and try on a different one and it's like you're seeing sunshine for the first time. And you realize shoes *can* be comfortable, you were just wearing the wrong one."

The longing he felt was sharp enough to make him blink back tears, yet he wasn't sure if he wanted to be like kir or to just possess that easy certainty. To *know*, once and for all, would be the greatest gift in the world. "But you were sure?" he persisted, studying kir face. "You never had any doubts?"

Kie laughed and scooped up the pile of broken arrows to carry back. "Of course I had doubts, Innes. I'd be sure one day and uncertain the next. It took me two years just to use my own pronouns, and I still mix them up sometimes in my head. Not just my own, either; I forgot Graeme's the other day and they had to correct me. I'm sure there are people out there who've never felt an inkling of doubt, but I'm not one of them. Wish I were."

"Then how do you ever know for certain?" Innes could hear the anguish in his voice. "How did you find the answer?"

Niven looked back at him, kir smile gentle under the shade of the trees. "Innes, I'll never *know* whether I'm right or wrong about what I am.

143

Nobody is going to take me aside after death and give me a self-awareness trophy to lord over all the other ghosts. There's no prophecy that will prove my gender is mine. But I'm happier with my new name and pronouns than I was before, and that's really all that matters. I've got one life to live and I've got an overlord to kill. Why be miserable if I don't have to be?"

"Sìne was here, looking for you." Ainsley looked up from her sewing as Innes walked in. The pins in her mouth made the words come out muffled and garbled, but for once Innes didn't grin. He pulled his boots off at the door in silence, setting them to one side so he wouldn't track mud everywhere. "Innes, did you hear me?" she asked, a little frown of concern creasing her forehead.

"Sorry. Yes, I heard." He shook his head and slumped into his chair across from her seat by the fireplace.

She frowned before returning to her stitching, the worry line settling on her brow just above the nose. "She's only just gone. If you leave now, you could catch her and bring her back for dinner. There'll be enough for a guest."

Innes shook his head and leaned back in his chair, imagining all the tension draining from his body. "No, thanks. I know what she wants; I just don't have an answer for her yet."

Silence stretched between them as Ainsley continued her stitching and waited for an elaboration that never came. "Do you want to talk about it?"

"No." He took a deep breath, closed his eyes and spoke in spite of himself. "She's got this wild plan that she thinks will work. There's a rumor that King Fearghas is planning a stay at a campsite about a day's walk north of here. They want to break ground on a new castle there. You're safer not knowing, but the broad outline calls for several barrels of pitch, some torches, and Graeme's old sheep costume they wear at holiday festivals."

She looked up from her work again, eyebrows raised high. "I like that sheep costume."

"You should; you made it for them."

Heavy silence stretched between them, full of unsaid words. Ainsley kept her eyes on the work in her hands and the careful stab of the needle as it went in and out along the hem. "Sìne wants you to go with her?"

Innes rubbed at the tension spot between his eyes, wishing his headache would go away. "Yes."

His mother nodded. "Do you want to go with her?"

He closed his eyes and leaned back further in his chair. "Yes? I think so." The uncertainty in his voice annoyed him, but he couldn't shake it. "Graeme and Niven are going with her. I think Carbry and Ùna, too. Màiri's been over the plan with a fine-toothed comb and even she thinks it stands a chance. I want to help."

Ainsley set her sewing down in her lap and looked at him, her eyes gentle. "So what's the problem?"

Innes couldn't look at her. "I'm afraid of messing it up." His voice was soft under the crackle of the fire. "No man can kill King Fearghas; everyone knows that much is true. Sìne, Graeme, Niven, Carbry, and Ùna: none of them is a man. But me? I don't know. I keep asking myself, over and over again, and I don't have an answer. Maybe I'd have one if the question wasn't so loaded by the prophecy."

"Mmm." Without looking at her, he imagined her fingers moving absently over her stitching as she chose her words; Ainsley was always careful when she spoke. "You think any one of those five could be the hero, but not you. You think you aren't good enough but they are."

He shook his head, opening his eyes to stare at the ceiling. "I don't know if one of them is the hero. Sìne doesn't have two living parents, unless there's a different father she doesn't know about somewhere, and Ùna has never known her birth parents at all. If adoptive parents don't count, then she's probably out of the running as well." He sighed. "But if I came along,

I feel I might taint the whole thing with my presence. Whatever I did could be chalked up to a man's effort, so it couldn't succeed. If I even *am* a man; I still don't know."

Ainsley let him sit in silence for a long while as the fire crackled down. She stood, stretching her legs, and moved to put another log on the pile, poking with the long iron to stir the embers into fresh life. "Innes, you say no man can defeat Fearghas, but the prophecy is 'no man of woman born'. If you weren't born of a woman, then it wouldn't matter whether you were a man or not. You'd satisfy the condition through birth."

Innes snorted. "Yes, if you'd found me under a cabbage patch, I'd be all set." Silence stretched between them and he opened his eyes to find her staring at him, one eyebrow raised. He frowned. "Did I miss something? You're my birth mother. Everyone says I look just like you; I'm not a fairy-born foundling."

She sighed and sat down opposite him, taking his hand in hers. Her smile was gentle but tinged with amusement, the way she looked when life took an unexpected turn without consulting her first. "You know, you've done so well with Graeme. I remember when they first asked us all to use 'they' and 'them'. You got it wrong for weeks, falling over yourself to apologize each time and just making it worse."

He winced in recollection. "In my defense, I hadn't met Niven yet," he pointed out, feeling sheepish. "And we still thought Ùna was a boy, because she hadn't corrected us. It was all very new to me."

Ainsley nodded, her hands warm and comforting on his. "I'm very proud of you. You've dealt so well with it all, and that's why I think—I *hope*—I can give you one more new concept to embrace. Innes, *I'm* a man."

Innes' first reaction was as unhelpful as it was automatic, unable to believe what he was hearing. "You're a man? Since when?" He stared at her as if he could divine her purpose from the lines on her face; was she saying this just to make him feel better about the prophecy? This wasn't like Graeme or Niven or Ùna, who were all his age or a little older. His mother was in her late forties, a time by which gender surely ought to be a settled matter.

Ainsley laughed, the sound soft over the crackle of the fire. "All my life, I think. I didn't always have the words for it, and for a long time I thought it was just my imagination or that everyone felt the way I did. I'm quite certain now that I'm male and always have been, but I was told otherwise for so long that I accepted I couldn't be."

"Does Father know?" Eoghan was powerful in the forge but gentle with people, soft and quiet-spoken; Innes couldn't imagine Ainsley wouldn't want to tell him something like this, but what if she'd been afraid of his reaction? What if Innes were the first person she'd told? He didn't want to keep secrets from Eoghan, but he knew as soon as the words left his mouth that this story wasn't his to tell.

She dispelled those fears with a level gaze. "Young man, have you ever known me to hold back from sharing my thoughts with your father?" He shook his head and she smiled, her eyes softening. "Sorry. I shouldn't call you a young man. Not until you tell me you are one."

He puffed out his cheeks and released a long, slow breath. He'd asked himself daily for years: *man or not?* The question was still important to him and he was no closer to an answer, but for the first time the weight behind it had shifted. He didn't need to know right now; he could take all the time he needed to find out.

"When I know, I'll tell you," he promised, feeling light-headed. "And... should I use 'he' for you? Are you my father? I mean, another one?"

Ainsley's smile was gentle. "I'll admit I haven't worked through all that yet. Maybe you could use it around the house? I'm not quite ready to come out and tell everyone in town. Mind you, if you *do* make a hero of yourself, I'll have to come out to satisfy everyone's curiosity." He chuckled at the idea.

"You know this doesn't necessarily make me the chosen one," Innes pointed out, raising an eyebrow. "It just means I'm not out of the running." He paused. "Is Father—I mean, Eoghan—a woman?"

His father laughed and leaned forward to kiss his forehead. "He is not. You are born of two men, sweetheart, whether or not you turn out to be one yourself, and we're both very much alive and very proud of you. Of course, you're more than welcome to double-check and ask him his gender over dinner. But, Innes, I want you to do something for me."

Innes looked up at him, searching eyes he'd known all his life: full of warmth and love for him, overflowing with confidence and pride in whatever he might do. "What's that?"

Ainsley squeezed his hands with gentle affection. "I won't tell you to go with your friends; only you can make that decision for yourself, Innes. What I want is for you to promise me you'll base your decision on the strength of Sìne's plan and your faith in the others to carry it out. Consider everything relevant, but don't doubt yourself and your value. You are my child, and you are special and loved. Whether you're a boy, or a girl, or both, or neither, or something else entirely, Eoghan and I will love you as we always have and always will."

The lump that constricted his throat was worth the pain for the relief he felt, the depth of which surprised him. Lunging forward, he almost fell from his chair in the rush to hug his father. His sweet, beautiful father, whose clever hands made such good clothes and who always had a joke to lighten Innes' spirits whenever he was down. Innes clung to him and his father embraced him back and he knew what he'd somehow known all along: they wouldn't love him any less if he didn't grow up to become a man. It felt so good to hear Ainsley say so.

His father held him for more heartbeats than he could count, stroking his hair and letting him weep. When Ainsley finally broke the silence, his voice was thick with tears of his own. "Does that mean you'll be going to find Sìne?"

Innes laughed a wet little cough of a laugh, sniffing as he wiped tears from his cheeks. "After dinner," he promised, looking up at his father with a wide grin. "I still want to check with Eoghan first, just to be sure. But afterwards, yes." He leaned up to kiss his father's cheek, memorizing the scent of tailor's chalk and smoke which always hung about Ainsley no matter how much he washed. Innes might lose his life trying to make the world better, but right now he had this moment to savor and it was enough.

"I love you, Father. I always will."

A gentle kiss ruffled his hair. "I love you, too. Fight well, and remember that I couldn't be more proud of you."

THE WISH-GIVER

Everyone in the kingdom knew about the wish-giver. The mother of all dragons had lived in her den on the hill as long as anyone could recall and was older than the most aged elders in the land. Her hill rose just high enough to overlook the nearby walled capital and the sprawling farmlands which surrounded the city. Some said the city itself, the shining jewel of the kingdom and its pride and joy, had been the first wish she granted to mankind.

For that was what the dragon did: she granted wishes. Those who were brave enough to take the path up the hill, face her outside her den, and call her out to battle could, if they defeated her in honorable combat, obtain their heart's dearest desire. From all corners of the kingdom challengers came, brave or foolhardy or both, undeterred by the knowledge that few won the day against the immortal beast.

Battling the dragon was not a risk to be taken lightly. Some knights limped home after their defeat, bloodied and broken. Many were devoured whole by the creature or, if they brought no squire to witness their defeat, were simply never seen or heard of again. Perhaps one in a thousand challengers were clever enough or strong enough or quick enough to best the dragon, and these rare winners were the stuff of legends.

150

These heroes and heroines whose tales were sung by the bards were frequently gentle people with good hearts and pure intentions. One wish saved a small village from starvation when its fields were set upon by a locust swarm. Another wish released a girl from marriage to a man who held her family's home as forfeit in a debt, so that she might be free to marry the bonny maiden whose wish released her. The most popular tale in the taverns was of a retired soldier who took up his sword one last time to wish for peace in his homeland. The dragon granted him a silver tongue with a talent for diplomacy; within a month after his battle with the wyrm a solution pleasing to both sides had been reached, ending a blood feud which had ravaged the land and its inhabitants for generations.

Drunken arguments raged cheerfully over the soldier's wish and the dragon's definition of 'peace', but that was what the dragon did: she looked into the hearts of mankind and gave what was desired, regardless of the wording. No victor ever complained about the outcome of their wish, and this was a comfort to the audiences of their stories; the creature wouldn't wriggle out of a fair defeat through word trickery. The dragon was lethal but fair, playing by rules she had set herself many centuries ago.

The path to the dragon's den was not a difficult one. The hill formed a gentle slope to the top, the track worn by so many boots taking that final march to dream or death. Farms sprawled between the hill and the city walls, supplying the capital with grain for their bread and grapes for their wine, and a small but thriving line of businesses catering to prospective wish-seekers abutted the foot of the hill. There were artists to sketch a final likeness, scribes to take down last words or a will and testament, and pleasure-workers to grant one night of bliss to men and women who might not see another sunset. Such were the good people who lived in the shadow of the wish-giving dragon, content to ply their trades, raise their families, and leave wild dreams to others.

Children played at the base of the hill on sunny days when their guardians washed and dried the family laundry and let the little ones out to play. They ran and shouted and laughed together, the children of the farmers and artisans mingling without reservation in their shared games. No one noticed the little fat-cheeked child who moved away from the larger group and toddled determinedly up the hillside.

The child was barely more than a baby, four summers old at most. They toddled easily up the hill, little legs propelling them up the soft earthen path without hesitation. Unruly hair sprang in every direction on their head and spilled down their back in beautiful frizzy waves, making the child seem younger than the length of their chubby limbs implied; no doubt the mother had resisted taming the child's hair out of a fond desire to keep them a baby for just a little longer. Soon the child's hair would be cut or braided, according to their gender.

Their gender was obvious at a glance, of course; the parents had swathed the child in yellow, the color of the sun, to set them apart from those children clothed in green, the color of grass and growing things. The colors determined how others interacted with the child, how the child was raised and educated, and which careers the child would be best suited to in life. Few positions were completely barred to a child because of their color— the yellow children *could* teach, nurse, or train warriors if they so chose, just as the green children *could* enter the army, bake, or run a shop if they wanted—but the colors would always guide them. Stories were sometimes told in the kingdom of other countries and other colors, or of countries with no colors at all, or places where colors could change at a whim, but few paid heed to such tales. Yellow and green made sense, having been set down as the standard as far back as anyone could remember.

Yellow was the color, too, of the dirt path leading to the dragon's den; a sandy yellow-brown where wish-seekers had trodden the earth until it was no longer suitable for growing things. The yellow-clothed child faded into the path as they approached their goal, unnoticed by the humans below as they raised the little wooden sword they had brought with them. Only when the shining dragon emerged from her cave at the sound of a shout,

152

the sun glinting from her polished emerald scales, did the adults at the foot of the hill finally notice the tiny warrior. Far below a woman screamed, her reedy voice carried away on the wind.

The queen of all dragons, the huge and majestic wish-giver, stood on four legs the size of tree trunks in the dazzling morning sunlight and gazed down upon the soft round child standing at the foot of her den. The little thing, barely more than a mouthful to the great beast, waved their toy in the air and howled what they must have surely *thought* sounded like a battle cry. Running forward, stumbling, correcting themselves and running again, the child eventually reached the left forefoot of the creature. A stab of the wooden sword at the massive leathery paw, and the blade stuck between talons the size of the child's torso.

A tense silence descended as only the child breathed, panting as they struggled to free the sword that was stuck fast. The dragon herself did not stir, nor did the knot of anxious watchers gathering at the foot of the hill to witness in helpless horror the certain death of one of their own. Still the child grunted and pulled, not noticing or caring for the audience below. There was only this one goal, their dream worth fighting for.

The dragon's voice broke the silence, booming at a deep pitch that carried on the wind to the city walls. "Thou hast pierced my weak spot, brave warrior. I am defeated, and one wish is thine that thou might spare mine own life in return. Speak thy desire that I might grant thy wish to thee."

Blinking up at the towering creature, the child stopped tugging at their blade as these words of surrender washed over them. Brown eyes open wide, they stared through a haze of dark curls; then the child inhaled a gulp of air and shouted as loudly as they could, trusting in volume to carry their words up to the faraway dragon.

"I want to be a girl!"

Silence again, now stunned rather than horrified; on the ground beneath the hill, heads turned back and forth as the watchers grappled with their surprise at both the unexpected victory and the wish that followed. The dragon's gaze did not falter, nor did the ancient creature blink; if anything, her reptilian eyes grew softer. Her voice still boomed but there was a gentleness in its timbre when she answered, abandoning the flowery words of her ancient ritual to address the tiny child.

"Little one, you *are* a girl."

The baby nodded at this, her lips pressed together in exasperation; the face of a child long made weary by the illogic of adults. "I know, but everyone down there calls me a boy! I want you to fix it!" A belated airy 'please' followed; a child's forgetful manners, inconstant as a playful spring breeze.

Staring down at her, the dragon nodded her ancient head in a slow, thoughtful bob. "Many things I can fix," she said, dipping her serpentine neck low to the ground until her head rested on the earth below and her eyes were almost level with the little petitioner. "Let me see your eyes, child. Tell me your heart's desire."

They spoke while the sun climbed to the highest point in its daily journey. The watchers strained to listen, but heard only the soft babyish cadence of the little girl in yellow and the low unintelligible rumble of the dragon as she questioned the child. Just when her parents were ready to faint from worry, the dragon began to wrap herself around the little one in the same way a cat might curl into a ball for a nap. A scream rose from the knot of watchers who moved to rush the hill with their pitchforks and carving knives, but the dragon's scales pulsated with an emerald light so bright that the humans fell back dazzled, covering their eyes.

Over yelps and cries, one sound floated above the cacophony: a child's happy giggle. As the adults rubbed at their eyes, they glimpsed the tail of the dragon slinking back into her hill, the light fading from her scales as she called a few final inaudible words to the girl behind her. One man had rushed ahead of the group and ascended further than the others before the blinding light struck; he later swore the dragon had said "Come again, if ever you have need of me." Then the great lizard was gone and the child was left behind.

She was unchanged, as far as the watchers could see. Her face was a child's face, her wild mane a child's hair. The soft, fat arms and legs that had carried her up the hill now brought her down with the same confidence. Her weeping parents fell on her, the father clutching the girl to his chest as her mother checked her hands and feet again and again for cuts, scrapes, and wounds that were not there. The child was safe and whole, unharmed by her experience and barely conscious of the stir she had caused with her morning's adventure. She beamed a warm smile at the watchers, pleased that they were happy.

"I'm a girl." She grinned at them from the comfort of her father's arms, her tone the easy one of a child who hopes finally to be listened to after all her trials and tribulations. "I'm a girl, and the dragon helped."

Faces stared back at the child in confusion, awe, and shock. Yet here and there were pockets of sympathy. The wish was unusual, even strange, but hadn't they heard wilder ones? They lived in the shadow of the dragon, many of them serving the wish-seekers and hearing their stories in the process. All their lives they had listened to the desires of men and women, selfish and selfless alike, each wish more outlandish than the last. One did not risk death at the claws of a dragon for anything less than the deepest desire of the heart.

In the face of all those needs and wants, was it so impossible that one child might wish to change... what? Her body? The clothes and colors which adorned her? What precisely had the little girl wished for in her whispered conversation with the dragon, and what had the ancient creature granted her? The watchers didn't know and the protective stances of the child's parents indicated the likely reaction if they were to ask.

The girl broke the silence again, brushing the untamed frizz of curls away from her face and yawning. "Can we eat now? I'm hungry. I want to go home, Papa."

Her father hugged the girl in his arms and kissed her hair. His voice was thick when he spoke, choking back the tears he hadn't dared shed when the child stood on the hill. Now that she was safe, his eyes watered and each word threatened to crack from the force of his relief.

"Of course you are, my brave girl; battling dragons is hungry work. Let's go home."

Note to the Reader

Thank you for reading this book! I hope you have enjoyed it and you are very welcome to leave a review or recommend this novel to a friend; reviews and recommendations are the lifeblood of indie authors and I cannot thank my reviewers enough for their kind words. If I may, I would like to insert a brief note on gender and ways to craft a review without harming other readers.

Many of the characters in the stories you have just read are transgender people, that is to say they are people whose gender does not match the gender assigned to them at birth. For example, Finndís is a trans woman who was erroneously assigned male at birth (AMAB). She was not 'born a boy', nor is she 'male', nor did she 'change' her gender at any point in her life; she has always been a girl, even if rest of the world has not always recognized that fact.

Please only refer to characters by their correct pronouns. For characters whose gender might be considered a 'spoiler', it would be better not to reference them at all in reviews rather than concealing their gender with incorrect pronouns. Thank you for being considerate; sensitive reviews for books with trans characters are easier for trans readers to navigate.

Bless you again for reading my work! More resources on transgender characters and how to write about them are available at GLAAD.org and Nonbinary.org for those who are interested. I owe a debt of gratitude to Vee (@FindMeReading) of GayYA.Org for sharing their poignant thoughts regarding how trans characters are handled in book reviews and how we can better serve our community.

Acknowledgements

I would not have had the idea for this collection of stories were it not for the friendship and mentoring I have received from authors Chelsea Cameron and Elliot Wake. Chelsea first suggested to me the idea of old fairytales written with transgender characters, and Elliot was a whirlwind of inspiration as he shared with me the achingly beautiful prose of his own transgender fairytale retelling project.

Nor would I have had the motivation to see this project through to completion were it not for my wonderful followers on Twitter and my blog, Ramblings. When I suggested the idea of combining trans characters with gendered prophecies and floated half a dozen one-liner summaries for the stories in this collection, hundreds of replies poured in urging me to write and offering to beta read. I was stunned by the strength of the response and realized there were people as hungry for these stories as I was.

Many of these wonderful volunteers stayed with me throughout the life of the project, and I am humbled and grateful for the work they've put into beta reading for me out of the goodness of their hearts. Those who consented to be thanked personally in these acknowledgements include: Aidan, Alex Conall, Bailey Grey, Bay Gaillard, Blythe "Collie" Collier, Dax Murray, Dee Shull, Jess Steyn, Jules Bristow, Kayla Scheiner, Krista Grace, Kristy Griffin Green, Maeve Baruk, Michael Mock, NB Talkendo, Roo McClay, Samantha Tillman, Serenity Dee, Stephanie S., Teagan L, Thomas Keyton, and Tracey P.

I owe, too, a debt of deep gratitude to the friends and colleagues who read and shaped this work prior to publication. Kristy and Thomas, my wonderful writing partners in addition to beta readers, touched every page of this book and are my dearest friends who keep me writing through hard times. My sensitivity readers Ava Mortier, Jay, Lex Townsend, Mazikeen Wagner, and Serenity Dee were each worth their weight in gold. Elaine Kennedy is the most patient of editors, and Carolan Ivey provided valuable coaching over my cover copy and blurb. Much of what is good in this book is due to these people; anything bad which remains is on my head.

Lastly, I have been privileged to work with amazing artists as part of this project. Cori Samuel, who narrated the audio book, has the voice of an angel and is a treasure; I joyfully wept to hear her bring my words to life. Anna Dittmann, who created the book cover, makes the most beautiful art and it was an honor to collaborate with her. Claribel Ortega, creator of the lovely teaser videos used in the book's marketing, brought vibrant movement to my words and is in every way a delightful person and friend. Writing this book with so many wonderful people has changed me for the better and I am grateful.

Thank you for reading and supporting me in my work. Blessed be.

About the Author

ANA MARDOLL is a writer and activist who lives in the dusty Texas wilderness with two spoiled cats. Her favorite employment is weaving new tellings of old fairy tales, fashioning beautiful creations to bring comfort on cold nights. She is the author of the Earthside series, the Rewoven Tales novels, and several short stories.

Aside from reading and writing, Ana enjoys games of almost every flavor and frequently posts videos of gaming sessions on YouTube. After coming out as genderqueer in 2015, Ana answers to both xie/xer and she/her pronouns.

Website: www.AnaMardoll.com
Twitter: @AnaMardoll
YouTube: www.YouTube.com/c/AnaMardoll

Made in United States
North Haven, CT
15 March 2022

17195691R00096